Gregory

and the

Grimbockle

BOOK SOUNDTRACK

Gregory and the Grimbockle is a signature
New Wrinkle Publishing publication,
created with its own book soundtrack!

To download your complimentary
copy of Gregory and the Grimbockle:
Original Book Soundtrack, visit
newwrinklepublishing.com/soundtracks

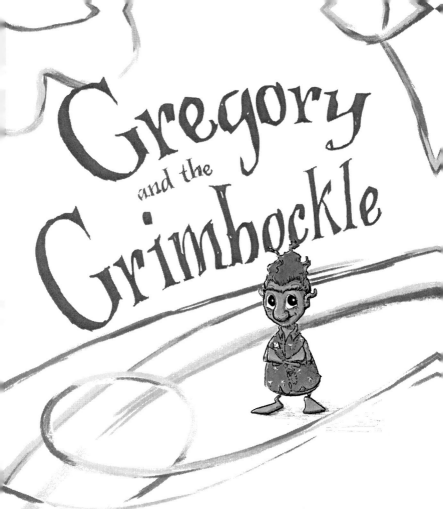

Gregory
and the
Grimbockle

Melanie Schubert

ILLUSTRATED BY
Abigail Kraft

BOOK SOUNDTRACK BY
Jared Kraft

NEW WRINKLE
PUBLISHING

Contents

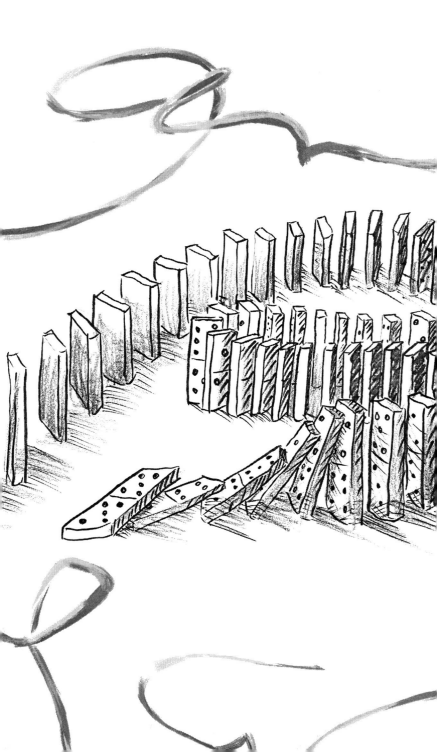

CHAPTER 1

The Mole

Gregory felt he must be the most unfortunate boy in the world. To start with, he had barely any friends. To make matters worse, over the past few years poor young Gregory had developed an enormous and oddly shaped mole above his top lip. It looked, from afar, exactly like a great dripping of chocolate that had melted down a table in the sun. A closer inspection revealed it to be very much like a rude bunch of dried-up grapes hanging from underneath Gregory's left nostril.

It was a strange mole indeed, and it wasn't entirely uncommon for a complete stranger to approach him on the street, lick his or her finger (or hanky), and rub at the drip mole heartily.

Gregory hated this. He disliked the attention. But even more, he loathed the stale smell of a stranger's saliva as it dried into a pale, smelly crust beneath his nose.

Even Gregory's own mother constantly forgot it was a mole. She would chase Gregory around the house for hours with her yellow-spotted tea towel, trying desperately to scrub it off. One day, she caught him and scrubbed the wretched thing so hard, it bled. Realising she'd made no progress in removing the stubborn splotch, she gave up. But often, still, he would catch her staring across the room at it, wringing her tea towel unhappily.

Aside from his mole, there wasn't much else in particular that stood out about Gregory. He was a typically stringy young boy of ten with scruffy black hair and dark, intelligent eyes that had a handsome slant to their corners like his father's. One of his feet was at least a size or two larger than the other, but no one except his family had known about it...that is, until his twelve-year-old sister, Marjory, had seen to it they did. Before long, the entire school knew.

"Big Foot," his classmates had dubbed him the moment they'd found out. After that, they stomped around the schoolyard, making horrible sounds at poor Gregory's expense.

Marjory didn't stop with his foot, either. She teased Gregory at every opportunity, and anytime something unfortunate happened to him, she would say, "*You* were born under a purple star." According to Marjory, this was an incredibly bad omen that meant Gregory would have to watch his back for life. Gregory didn't particularly believe in omens, but even so, any mention of purple stars made his skin prickle.

His most recent mole encounter was with Ethel, the grumpy old woman who lived down his street. She was at least a hundred years old, maybe more, and had already received two letters from the Queen of England, which had led her to believe she was honorary royalty.

When Gregory was much younger, Marjory had convinced him that old Ethel was a witch who boiled little boys like him for supper. This had always made him run hard and fast whenever he'd spotted old Ethel coming his way, and even now, he was a bit jumpy whenever she was about.

Much like his mother, old Ethel had something of a vendetta against Gregory's mole. Ethel seemed convinced that Gregory was just a dirty little boy who couldn't keep his face clean and appeared to have made it her mission in life to try to, as she put it, "Get that mess sorted!"

Gregory wondered how old Ethel supposed he managed to put a glob of dirt on his face in the exact same shape and place every day. Regardless, he tried his very best to keep out of her way as much as was humanly possible. Yet, on this particular day, he had been preoccupied the moment she'd pounced. He'd happened to notice the neighbourhood tomcat up high in a maple tree and was trying to decide if it was stuck or simply hunting the pigeons that came to roost for the evening in the branches. Before he'd even sensed her presence, Ethel's hand had shot out from the centre of a thick hedge beside him and tried to yank Gregory's mole clean off his face. When he'd cried out in pain and darted away, she had chased him all the way down the street, cane and all, screeching, "Come back here, you cheeky bloomberbine!"

Gregory wasn't sure what a bloomberbine was, but he'd felt offended all the same.

He stood by the mirror at home now, dabbing his poor bleeding mole with a cotton ball. The cotton should have felt soft, but with the mole cracked and bleeding the way it was, it felt like sandpaper.

Heaving a great sigh, he moved the cotton away and began to inspect the damage. Now that the bleeding had subsided, he could clearly see a great, jagged crack torn right through the centre of the mole. Up close, it looked a lot like the picture on the wall in his science class of a giant fissure out in the desert of Mexico.

He gave another sigh, pulled a face at himself in the mirror, and muttered under his breath about the craziness of old ladies and the danger of distractions.

By now, he was feeling very sorry for himself and, having already had dinner alone before his twilight walk, felt no need to leave his room again that night. Now, it may seem curious that a boy of ten should be out by himself so late, eating dinner alone and putting himself to bed when he pleased. But Gregory's family members were all rather self-absorbed and had never paid him much attention at all—not unless one counted making fun of his feet and attempting to scrub off his mole.

From the earliest he could remember, Gregory had been fending for himself. Making his own lunches, doing his own laundry... This was not to say his parents had mistreated him, necessarily, but his father was never around, and as for his mother, when she wasn't obsessively cleaning the house, her rear was usually firmly glued to the sullen-looking couch parked right in front of the telly.

Her favourite show was an afternoon soap called *Vows of Our Fathers*. When it was on, Gregory's mother never got up for anything—not even toilet breaks. This both impressed and disgusted Gregory, who had taken to leaving out a plate of biscuits just beyond her reach whenever her show was on to see if he could trick her into getting up. He hadn't yet succeeded.

Giving his wounded mole a final, cautious dab with the cotton, he leaned forward to drop the used ball into the small bin that sat at the base of the mirror stand. Right at that moment, he noticed something odd about his face. Something was hanging from his mole. Something small. Something black. Something...long.

Just a hair, thought Gregory, though his heart skipped a beat as he reached out to grab it. When he pulled back his fingers to inspect, he found them empty, but so, too, was the mole crack.

It probably fell to the floor, he thought before throwing himself straight into bed. He hadn't felt sleepy, but in no time at all, he was fast asleep.

If he had been awake, he might have caught sight of that long, black something rising out, once again, from his mole. Then, if he had looked harder, he might have even noticed that it was less like a hair and more suspiciously like the tentative antenna of an insect, testing the air with quivering lashings.

If he had continued looking, he would have seen the skin around the mole begin to shiver and ripple, then the mole itself begin to bulge and stretch outward like a bubble. Soon, he would have seen two beady eyes on the end of a strange-looking head peeking out, regarding Gregory's nostrils with distaste.

With a push and a wriggle, a fearsome creature began to hoist itself onward and outward from Gregory's mole, like a baby snake emerging from its flexible eggshell. As the creature exited the mole, something strange began to happen. The head (which at first had been quite tiny) began to swell and grow, as did the rest of the body.

By the time the creature had fully popped out, it was about the size of a regular pantry mouse. However, illuminated by the moonlight as it was, it looked far more like a frighteningly large cockroach—except for the back half of the creature, which was raised up and coloured a light, milky shade of purple.

The cockroach creature froze stiff, save its antennae, which were flicking about like whips, and its eyes darting madly around the room. Then, with a final flick of its antennae, it scuttled quickly down the side of Gregory's cheek, raced across the pillow, and took a flying leap from the edge of the mattress over to the bedside table.

This story might have ended here had all gone well. But it is about to take a twist and turn in that certain spectacular way that the most excellent stories do.

The creature landed fair and fine on its feet, but, alas, it was Tuesday, and on Tuesdays, Gregory's mother waxed all of the furniture. This meant that the moment those legs hit the shiny veneer of the table, all six of them slid out from underneath the poor beast, and it began skidding straight across the surface, eventually tumbling onto the floor.

Under normal circumstances, this wouldn't have been a terrible problem, for a falling insect makes barely a sound. But by a terrible stroke of luck, the creature happened to fall right on the worst place it could have.

You see, having almost no friends, Gregory spent a lot of time alone. The more time he spent alone, the better he became at entertaining himself. His latest obsession was dominos. He had hundreds, perhaps even thousands of them, lined up all around his room and had just finished linking the last of them together before dinner.

He had planned to knock them down right after his twilight walk, but his encounter with old Ethel had put him in a foul sort of mood, and he had decided to save the grand cascade for another, less offensive sort of day.

The domino chain began by the foot of the bedside table, which is precisely where the cockroach creature fell. Alas, it triggered an almighty cataclysm of dominos dropping, which, in turn, woke Gregory up.

CHAPTER 2

The Grimbockle

Gregory didn't shout or prance about the way most ten-year-olds might if their prized work of art had just been knocked down. No, he'd had far too many, more unfortunate things happen to him in his lifetime to be particularly surprised by this sort of incident. Instead, he simply sat up in his bed, making barely a sound, and waited silently as his masterpiece came tumbling down.

In a dark corner at the base of the table, the cockroach creature was stealthily creeping away as if hoping the *clack-clack-clack*ing of the dominos would cover its escape. But Gregory wasn't watching the dominos at all. He knew exactly where each one stood and could gauge in an instant the place the toppling had begun. He peered through the darkness to the spot where he knew something was moving while he felt for the cold metal of the aluminium flashlight he kept hidden under his pillow.

This was no child's toy. It was the KEENVIZZ 8000—a special tactical flashlight for which Gregory had squirrelled away every penny since he was five. His parents had never given him any money, of course. But every now and then, when the lemon tree out front bore more lemons than anyone knew what to do with, Gregory had been permitted to use the extra lemons that fell to the ground to set up a lemonade stand at the end of the street.

He'd hoarded a small fortune in the end, and right when he'd had exactly enough, he had gone straight to the hardware store and bought the flashlight he'd been admiring for years.

Had his parents ever found him with such an

expensive trinket, they would most certainly have confiscated it immediately. And so, to keep his special flashlight safe, Gregory carried it with him by day and tucked it under his pillow by night.

It didn't look particularly special. It was small, short, and painted a plain dusty black. But it was a very clever thing, the sort of flashlight that didn't need any kind of batteries or plugs to work. Should it ever go flat, one simply had to give it a quick shake to recharge, and, hey-ho, the lights were back on in an instant. It was also waterproof and had a dangerously bright beam that could pierce through almost anything. Once, on a school camping trip, Gregory had seen some of his classmates shining their flashlights through their palms to make the tops of their hands glow red. When he'd tried this with the KEENVIZZ 8000 later that night, the light had been so bright, it had come through his hand and out the other side— bright enough to shine through the wall of his tent and wake up the girls in the tent next door.

Once he had his flashlight in hand, Gregory searched with his finger for the rubber end, then aimed for the precise spot where he thought the tremor had started.

He knew it wasn't Marjory who had knocked the dominos down. He could hear her unholy snores bouncing off the walls and rattling the windows in her bedroom.

Releasing half a breath, Gregory gave a quick, hard click to the button at the flashlight's end. The cockroach creature was illuminated instantly, surrounded by a bright circle of light exactly like a prima ballerina in the spotlight, centre stage. It scrambled frantically left...then right...but seemed trapped by the circle of light as if its edges were a solid concrete wall.

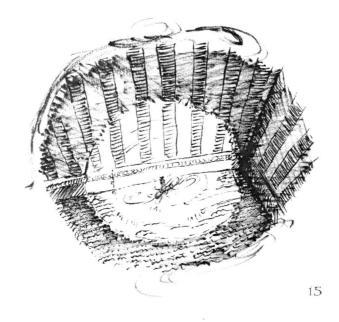

It became quite apparent that it was, indeed, a cockroach. Also obvious now was the strange purple man sitting frozen in fright on its back, stunned by the dazzling glare of the KEENVIZZ 8000.

"Egads!" hissed Gregory under his breath in surprise.

Hearing him speak, the small purple man fell forward, whispering secret commands urgently to its steed. Instantly, the cockroach leapt to life and, in the blink of an eye, scuttled straight under the bed.

Gregory scrambled over to the other side of the mattress just in time to catch them with his light. Once again, the cockroach seemed baffled by the brightness, scurrying from side to side so many times (and so quickly) that it soon grew tired. Finally, it stopped and cowered in the middle of the light, shivering like a small, frightened animal out in the rain.

Realising it was trapped, the tiny purple man fainted, falling right off its trembling cockroach steed and tumbling onto the floor.

Suddenly, it was Gregory's turn to freeze as heavy footsteps came pounding down the hall.

"Gregory!" came his mother's cranky voice down the corridor. "What's going on in there?"

He clicked off the flashlight and leapt under the blankets into his bed just as the door flew open and his mother strode into the room.

She scanned the room thoroughly and noticed the fallen dominos. Then, seeing Gregory asleep in his bed, she quietly closed the door and returned to her room. As soon as he heard her footsteps disappearing down the hall, Gregory threw back the blankets and shone his flashlight under the bed.

Nothing was there.

He flashed the light around the room, scanning the hundreds of fallen dominos, but saw nothing.

Clicking off the light, he closed his eyes and strained his ears to listen in the dark. At first, he heard nothing but the dull rumble of Marjory, still snoring in the other room. He could hear the thin branches of the willow outside scratching gently on the window. A loud dripping sound was coming from somewhere in the house. Other than that, the night was still.

He was about to give up when he heard the dominos shifting once again. Immediately, he cast his light over to where he'd heard the noise. There he saw the sorry sight of the cockroach trying to walk backwards, dragging the little purple man along with its antennae wrapped around both its legs. As soon as the light fell upon it, the cockroach froze, and the little purple man began to stir.

"Ow...," it moaned, rubbing its head.

Gregory kept his light fixed on them.

The little purple man squinted nervously into the blinding light.

"What on earth is it?" wondered Gregory, thinking aloud.

"I is nothing! Nothing at all!" said the creature, trying to hide behind the cockroach.

"But you're not nothing at all. I'm seeing you right now...unless I'm still asleep...."

"Yes!" said the creature hopefully. "You *is*

asleep. You is dreaming me up."

"It doesn't feel like a dream," said Gregory, pinching himself hard. "Ouch!" he muttered, rubbing the injured spot. "Definitely not a dream. What on earth are you?"

"I-I is a Bockle," said the creature valiantly, though its voice trembled more than a little.

"A what now?"

"A Bockle."

"What in the world is a Bockle?" Gregory almost shouted, but he forced the words to a whisper. (It simply would not do if any of his family woke up. As it was, he was amazed his mother hadn't shaken him awake to ask about the dominos falling.)

"A Bockle is a Bockle just as a hoo-man is a hoo-man," said the creature, flicking its eyes around the room as if it thought someone might be listening.

"I see," said Gregory, not understanding at all.

"But I is the *Grim*bockle," the creature said, as though it were important.

"So, that's your name? Is it a boy's name?" Gregory asked.

"Yes, it is my name, but I is not a boy. I is a Hebockle. Now, please," it said in a slightly withered voice, "you is blinding us with your ferocious little sun."

"Little sun?" said Gregory before realising it must mean the flashlight. Carefully, he slid off the edge of the bed and flicked on the star-shaped nightlight. At the same time, he clicked off the KEENVIZZ 8000, freeing the Grimbockle from its intangible prison. The nightlight had been a gift from his sister (one of the only things she had ever given him), though it was less a gift than a gag, the colour of the star being purple.

Still, Gregory quite liked it, and as he flicked it on now, a gentle purple glow emanated from it softly, coating the room in a dusky purple light. He lowered himself down and lay flat until his chin came to rest on the floor in front of the tiny purple Grimbockle.

"Hello," he said, not knowing what else to say.

"Oh!" said the Grimbockle, wringing its hands and pacing beside the cockroach. "I is going to be in a pesky big mess over this! A pesky big mess indeed!"

The Grimbockle was off its six-legged mount now, and Gregory could finally begin to see what a strange little creature it was. Its basic shape wasn't too far removed from human, but its body was like a tiny purple onion and seemed to hover above its webbed feet, which looked remarkably similar to those of a duck. It's hands were much the same, but looked somehow more flexible, like a spider monkey's, with soft purple webbing in between the fingers.

Its skin was a light milky purple that appeared to emit a slight glow of its own, different from the one coming from the nightlight.

Its nose was large and bulbous, and sitting right above it was a set of great round eyes, dark as night and seeming to take up half the creature's face.

It had a shock of hair that was a darker shade of purple than its body, and it swayed on its own as the Grimbockle moved around, reminding Gregory of seaweed floating in the sea.

The only clothing it wore was a faded red shirt with white palm trees printed over it. The front of the shirt was buttoned, but down near the bottom hung the round and portly stomach of the Grimbockle, straining against the buttons.

Around its neck, it wore a long rope of light pink pearls. The entire effect was rather amusing, and Gregory couldn't help but smile a little at the creature's appearance.

"Oh," it twittered, holding its head between its hands and continuing to pace, "I is finding myself in rotten stinky trouble when the big bosses is hearing about this foul, messy muck up! I is being squished! I is being squashed! I is becoming the frog in the water pot's hot boiling stew!"

CHAPTER 3

The Exoodle Threads

"I'm sure you'll be fine," said Gregory. "After all, it's not as though I'm going to be running off telling people I saw you."

"You isn't?" said the Grimbockle, lifting its head up hopefully.

"Well, who would I tell? People would think I was mad." He paused. "But what exactly *is* a Bockle?"

The Grimbockle regarded him silently for a moment with its great liquid eyes.

"Bockles," it said sagely, "is controlling thoughts."

"Controlling what?" said Gregory, aghast. "You mean like...mind control?"

"Oh no! Nothing dark or damp like that. We is not controlling hoo-man thinkings at all. We is just...fixing things."

"What kinds of things?"

"Ours," said the Grimbockle, puffing its chest out proudly, "is a special kind of work. *We* is controlling the threads."

As soon as it said this, the Grimbockle looked nervous, and, once again, its eyes began to dart around the room as if it feared someone or something might be listening.

"The threads," repeated Gregory dumbly, wondering again if he were actually awake. He yanked a few hairs from his arm just to make sure. "Owww!" he hissed, shaking his arm and terrifying the Grimbockle, who jumped two inches into the air. (Now, two inches may not sound like much, but actually the Grimbockle had jumped almost twice its own height.)

"Oh, sorry," said Gregory, chuckling a little.

The Grimbockle nodded, recomposing itself.

"The threads," it said, continuing, "is the weaving, winding fibres that is connecting hoo-mans from one to the other."

"Like string phones?" wondered Gregory, picturing an immense contraption made of intertwined cup-phones.

"Exac-tilly! But these is teensy-weensy threads. Threads that is een-visible to the hoo-man eyes. Threads that is connecting feelings from one hoo-man to another."

"How do you mean?" asked Gregory, mystified.

The Grimbockle looked around the room again. It seemed to be contemplating whether it should continue to explain or attempt another escape.

"It's okay. I promise not to tell anyone," Gregory assured the Grimbockle.

Hesitating for a moment, the Grimbockle continued. "Is you ever feeling...sad? So sad that tears is trickling down your cheekses and falling into your lap? But then, right at that moment, the phone is ringing off the hook, and who should be calling but your favouritest cousin!"

Gregory felt a tingle up his spine. You see, he had only two real friends in the world, and one of them was his cousin, Pat. He lived in another country now, but more times than he could count, when he had been feeling especially low, Pat had called.

"So, what do you do with these threads?"

The Grimbockle waddled a little closer to Gregory, looked straight up at him, and said, "Sometimes, the threads is breaking. When threads is breaking, important messages is often getting lost. This is most disas-trus," it said, shaking its head. "Most disas-trus indeed."

The Grimbockle spoke in a lovely, trilling way, and it was rather a pleasure to listen to it. Its voice sounded almost musical, like tiny bells rustled by an ocean breeze.

"Friend-ships is ending," it continued, "brothers and sisters is having tiffs. Even dogs-es and cats-es is getting miffy at their hoo-mans when the strings is breaking."

"Even cats and dogs are connected?" Gregory asked in surprise.

"Of course cats-es and dogs-es!" said the Grimbockle, with serious eyes. It stared at Gregory solemnly, making him feel as though he'd somehow asked a ridiculous question. "Some hoo-mans is being able to attach even stronger threads to cats-es and dogs-es than they is able to on other hoo-mans."

"Why?" asked Gregory, curious.

"Cats-es and dogs-es is bathing much less. Threads is growing long and strong when creatures is not bathing much. Hoo-mans is bathing much too frequently, so we is always having to do maintenance work on hoo-man threads."

"I see," said Gregory (although he was having a terrible time understanding what the Grimbockle was telling him).

The Grimbockle seemed suddenly forlorn. "I is having one especially sad teen right now, far, far away from his mum-sie. She is needing to ring him, but she has forgotten. She is off in Calee-for-nee-ya swimming with sea otters."

"How horrid!" said Gregory.

"Yes. Seawater is doing especially nasty things to exoodles."

"Exoodles?"

"*Exoodles* is what threads is being called," said the Grimbockle grandly. "Threads is named exoodles because they is already *exooding* out of hoo-mans. We is just attaching them and making sure they is going where they is supposed to be going on their merry little ways. They is reminding Bockles of noodles the way they is wriggling about. They is exooding noodles."

"So you don't actually make the threads?"

"Isn't you listening?" said the Grimbockle, waggling its webbed hand in Gregory's face. "They is exooding from hoo-mans already. We is not being able to make them even if we is wanting to. Exoodles is curious, mystical things. Even Bockles is not fully being able to understand them. Now, enough of all these yarn-spinning tales," it said with a little huff. "We is moving forward to the present! I is not having any moments left to dally about."

"Riiiight," said Gregory. "So, you have to go and fix the threads for that mother swimming with the sea otters?"

"Exac-tilly. I is running out of day and time. I is leaving this particular case too long, so I is being in a fearsome fast rush. This is why I is tumbling off the table and onto the floor in the first place."

"It's rather lucky I didn't squash you when I stood up," said Gregory.

"Yes. Lucky indeed. Some poor trumpeting teen-ster would have been very lonely tonight if that was happening."

CHAPTER 4

The Painting of Peepers

The Grimbockle twittered some orders to the cockroach as it climbed onto its back. Immediately, the cockroach leapt to attention, then skittered about the room in a haphazard manner as though it were searching for something.

A couple of seconds later, it froze stock-still and pointed one of its long, slender antennae straight forward like a tiny six-legged hunting dog. The Grimbockle climbed off gingerly and picked at something in the air.

"Oh, my six sainted aunts!" it croaked, surveying the damage.

Gregory couldn't see anything but moved over anyway in the hope that he would. A closer view revealed nothing. "There's nothing there!" he said, disappointed.

"If everyone is seeing exoodles hanging about like spidey-webs, they is most certainly yanking them off bi-weekly at least. I is thinking there is not being nearly enough Bockles for fixing up all of the damage. Bockles is barely keeping up as it is!"

"But where are they?" said Gregory looking around.

"Exoodles is exooding out from the exact same places where Bockles is coming and going in hoo-mans."

"And where's that?" wondered Gregory aloud.

"Exoodles is coming out of moles."

"Ohhh...," said Gregory, feeling sick.

"Exoodles is always coming from moles, and moles is always coming for exoodles. Whenever you is seeing a new mole that is popping up on your body, you can bet your billy's bottom that a new exoodle has been borned, straight out from this humpy crumpy portal of skin."

"But wait...you said Bockles are using the moles for their comings and goings as well? Are you saying there's a Bockle living in each of my moles right now? *Were you in my mole?*"

An unbearable wave of itchiness swept over Gregory as soon as he'd said this, and he couldn't

help reaching up to give his giant mole a scratch. This he regretted instantly, the mole still tender from old Ethel's evening attack.

"No. Bockles is only living in larger moles, and only temper-air-rilly. Bockles is using hoo-man moles like holee-day houses, when we is having rumbling, bumbling amounts of work to do."

"What about people who have no moles?"

"In these misfortunate circumstances, Bockles is having to use *other* places for our comings and goings."

"What kinds of places?" said Gregory nervously.

"Nostrils, mouth-ses, even eyeballs when we has to."

Gregory felt faint as the Grimbockle continued. "But large moles is preferable. Large moles is making very cuddling, cushiony homes."

Gregory was still feeling squeamish, but by now, his curiosity was stronger. "What about the smaller moles? What are they good for?"

"We is not using them for living in. Small moles is only being formed for exoodles and is popping up fresh all the time."

"How, err, often would you say they pop up?"

"This is depending greatly on the hoo-man. Some sweet souls is being covered head to toe in wonderful specklings of freckles and spots. Freckly hoo-mans is always delightful and is always making lots of exoodles quickly with everyone in sight. We is not having to do so many fix-up jobs on freckly hoo-mans."

"But how do they form?"

"New exoodles is forming over time and with hoo-man interactings. This is why babies is being made with almost no moles at all. Babies is coming fresh and frisky from the womb without a single mole in sight."

"What about birthmarks?" said Gregory, mystified.

"Birthmarks," said the Grimbockle knowingly, "is for Trumpleforgs. Everyone is knowing that."

"Trumpleforgs? But what—"

"Come now! I is putting a stop to all this chittery-chattsing. I is having to get back to work before time is running out on us!"

Gregory watched the Grimbockle silently for a while as it used its webbed hands to scoop at something Gregory couldn't see. Suddenly, he had a thought. "Say, why was this other boy's exoodle here in my room to begin with?"

"When I is finding a thread that needs a fixing, of course I is bringing the middle bits with me. Then you and your mole is acting as an anchoring point for the thread being fixed, so I is finding it quickly when I is needing it again. Anchoring points is essential for in-between fixings. Otherwise, Bockles is having untold troubles trying to find the exoodles we is working on again."

"Well, I suppose that makes sense," said Gregory, touching his mole lightly again.

"It is making much more sense than less. But sadly, you is always having your mole plucked and scrubbed, and my anchored exoodles is getting damaged almost daily. This is giving me bumbling loads of extra work to fix up. This particular muckabout must be taking me at least an hour to fix tonight, and I is still needing to get over to Calee-for-nee-ya."

"Sorry," said Gregory. "People are always plucking and scrubbing at my mole. I wish they wouldn't, but wishing hasn't gotten me anywhere so far. I thought about yanking it clean off with dental floss around a doorknob, the way you would with a loose tooth, except the last time my father did that to my sister, the tooth wasn't quite ready and, well...it made quite a mess. I can't seem to get that out of my head, even if it is a mole and not a tooth."

The Grimbockle made a face as if picturing the gruesome scene. "I is imagining it would be making an ucky mucky mess indeed."

"Yes. Well, I decided not to risk it," said Gregory. "Having a mole's not so bad after all. Besides, I'm rather glad I didn't get rid of it, now I've met you."

"I is also being glad this did not happen," said the Grimbockle, looking disturbed.

"I do rather wish I could see them, though— the exoodle threads," Gregory added.

"You is seeing them if you is wanting to. If you is bringing your twinklers over to me, I is painting them now, and you is seeing everything."

Gregory twisted his face as he considered the offer. While the idea of seeing the exoodles excited him, this was a strange little creature that he had only just met, so he wasn't sure he could—or should—trust it.

The Grimbockle wore a stranger expression still.

"What is it?" said Gregory, curious.

"I is never painting the peepers of a hoo-man before. I is not sure it is allowed."

Now that the Grimbockle appeared to be having second thoughts, all hesitation on Gregory's part vanished. He wanted so badly to have his eyes painted that the palms of his hands and the bottom of his feet began to sweat.

"Oh, please!" he whispered, as loudly as he could.

The Grimbockle, seeming satisfied somehow, jumped back on its cockroach steed and nudged its sides gently so it began moving slowly over to Gregory's face. Then, as if it were nothing, it climbed onto Gregory's cheek and began to move vertically straight up his face. This felt very ticklish, and Gregory had to fight the urge to slap both the cockroach and the Grimbockle. It took great concentration and incredible control of every muscle and nerve in his body. Even still, he couldn't help but release a dull shudder from his core, and the hairs on his body leapt to attention the way they did whenever his sister talked about purple stars.

Soon, the Grimbockle and its cockroach had made their way right up to the ridge of Gregory's nose and paused there for a moment. They were so close that Gregory felt he must be going cross-eyed, and it made him feel quite dizzy. More dizzying still were the antennae of the cockroach, which tickled poor Gregory's eyelids and made him blink madly.

"You has to stop blinking, or we is ending up knocked-off, as you hoo-mans is saying."

Gregory strained his eyes open until they watered. He found, in the end, that he could only succeed at this by focusing on the glowing purple nightlight.

"Is you ready?"

"I guess so," said Gregory, not sure what to expect.

He heard something like a tiny tin of paint being pried open, then smelt a strong whiff of something that reminded him very much of the smell that came out of the kitchen whenever his mother was going through one of her green smoothie crazes.

He fought the urge to ask what it was and instead remained silent.

"Carrot Juicy," said the Grimbockle, as if sensing the question. "Everyone is knowing freshly juiced carrots is being especially wonderful for the eyes, and this is being made from special carrots that Bockles is cultivating magically for years and years. Okay, now, open your squinters bright!"

Gregory strained his eyes open, as wide as he could, while the Grimbockle lay a quick coating of the Carrot Juicy over the surface of his eyes. It felt a little bit scratchy but cool and wet. A few seconds later, a hard and intense ball of pressure began building behind his eye sockets.

He tried to be brave, but he couldn't prevent his eyes from clamping shut. Nor was he able to stop the single tear that squeezed out from each during the process.

"You is being very brave," came the Grimbockle's voice. "I is seeing full grown Bockles crying like childrens and buckling at their spindlers after their first coating."

"I can't imagine why," said Gregory, rubbing his eyelids carefully. "How long do you suppose

it'll take? For the eye-coating to work, I mean."

"It is never taking long. No. Not long at all."

Once the pain had subsided, Gregory opened his eyes to the soft dark of the room, which seemed a bit enchanted in the purple glow of the nightlight. For a second, he thought he saw something shimmering in the corner of his eye, but it darted away the instant he tried to focus on it.

The Grimbockle had gone back to work on the floor now and had pulled out a work belt of oddly shaped tools. They seemed rather like the sort a dentist used for drilling in one's mouth, and the very look of them made Gregory's molars ache.

As it worked, the Grimbockle began to hum, and soon it was swaying side to side and singing a strange and piercing little ditty.

Oh, the exoodles connecting us all,
they fly through the air, like noodles in fall.
They is festively luscious and hidden like mice,
but fear not, my dumpling; exoodles is nice!

To Gregory, the song made no sense at all, but he found it funny all the same. The image of noodles flying through the air was especially amusing, and he was forced to stifle a laugh at the word "dumpling."

"But Grimbockle," said Gregory, blinking his newly coated eyes, "there's something about all of this I don't understand."

Without saying a word, the Grimbockle glanced up from its work to regard him for a moment.

"If there are millions of all these exoodle threads floating about..."

"Gazillions," corrected the Grimbockle.

"Right. Well, if there are gazillions of exoodles floating around, how come nobody ever notices them? Even if they are invisible, surely people would be getting tangled up all the time?"

The Grimbockle stopped what it was doing and looked up at Gregory intently. "Has you ever been feeling a long hair tickling at your back, but you is never finding it?"

"Well...yes."

"Is you ever seeing glimpses of squiggles in the corners of your twinklers but then they is disappearing in a snippety blink?"

"Of course, but—"

"And has you ever thought you is walking through spidey-webs, but you is never seeing them no matter how hard you is trying?"

By now, Gregory had fallen silent.

"Exoodles!" shouted the Grimbockle in triumph. "Sometimes, hoo-mans is getting so twisty and wound up in extra exoodles that they is feeling gloomy blue and heavy all day long."

"Exoodles can do that, too?"

"Oh-so certainly! Too many unnecessary exoodles is making hoo-mans feel overwhelmed. They is only feeling better when they is getting some spiffy good acky-punksha on their spines!"

"Acupuncture? Why's that?"

"Acky-punksha," said the Grimbockle carefully, "is breaking off all the unimportant threads and sending them off to the atmosphere. Acky-punksha-rists is understanding better than Bockles which threads is important for keeping and tumbling off all the others."

"Really? So acupuncture is the answer, then?"

"Of course!"

It was all very curious, and every time one of his questions was answered, Gregory would think of another.

"How long have you been doing this, Grimbockle? And how did the exoodles stay in check before the Bockles came along?"

The Grimbockle tilted his head to the side as he considered the question, "Hmmm...perhaps only a thousand years or so, I is thinking. Before that, people is not going so far away from each other all the time, so exoodles was finding their own ways happily home."

"Are you saying people shouldn't travel?"

"You is full of questions, isn't you? And per-posterus things you is asking as well! Travel is strengthening great many other bits and bobbles in hoo-mans. Oh, yes.

A travelling hoo-man is in its own right delightful indeed. You is misunderstanding my meanings. I is simply saying that hoo-mans is needing to make certain their exoodles is sumptuous and strong before they is going so far away. Many travelling hoo-mans is actually having even *stronger* exoodles than homebound hoo-mans. This is because travelling hoo-mans is often ending up somehow understanding exoodles even though they is never seeing them."

Nothing the Grimbockle said made any sense to Gregory. It was all so odd and mysterious. But since he was talking to a little purple creature that rode on a cockroach, he figured he might as well believe what it was saying.

Before he was able to mull for very long, a quivering wriggle of movement caught his eye, right in the blind spot of his vision. He felt whatever it was would certainly disappear the moment he went to look at it, but he moved his head reflexively all the same.

When he turned around, he found he was looking at a tiny paintbrush and tin, which the Grimbockle had coated his eyes with not five minutes before. The paint bucket and brush themselves were made of something transparent, like crystal, which meant Gregory could see straight into the bucket, which was filled with bright orange fluid. But it wasn't the bucket that had caught his attention. Right above the bucket, something was moving—something long and lithe that wriggled and squiggled about.

"Oh-ho, you is seeing something already, is you not?" said the Grimbockle without looking up from its work. "Soon, you is seeing more."

CHAPTER 5

Gregory Joins the Maintenance Team

All at once, Gregory could see them. They hung like great threads of yarn spun across the room, glistening in the colours of the rainbow, like a spider web in the sunlight after rain. Almost immediately, Gregory noticed two especially thick exoodles coming out from his own body. Lifting his shirt, he discovered both were anchored firmly to medium-sized freckles by his belly button.

He knew, instinctively, that one of these threads was for his cousin, Pat, and the other was for his friend Clarence, in New Zealand.

Gregory didn't know how he knew this, but it just came to him like some sixth sense. There were other threads coming off him, too, but these were wispy, thin, and frail by comparison.

"Oh! Now those is some lovely strong exoodles indeed," said the Grimbockle approvingly. "I is never needing to conduct maintenance work on those two."

"What about the others?" said Gregory.

He reached out his hand to try and grab one, but as soon as his hand came close, the wispy, thin threads jumped away like opposite ends of a magnet repelling each other.

"Those is needing work. I is often having to reattach many of those. Especially your sister-ling and parental exoodles. Sometimes an exoodle is not needing to be reattached at all and is simply floating away on its lonesome. You is not needing to keep threads for every frog and dog, after all."

Gregory was proud his exoodles for Pat and Clarence were so strong, though he did feel a little sad as well. He didn't like his family exoodles being in such a sorry state, even if his family was all a little nutty.

The Grimbockle, who was still working, began singing another song.

> Rain is raining pigs and frogs,
> rain is making hoo-man bogs.
> When the rain is falling down,
> why does insects never drown?

For the first time, Gregory noticed the exoodle the Grimbockle was working on. It was thick but limp, and it trailed along the floor in a sad little S shape. Gregory thought it looked like a long, fat earthworm that had wriggled out of the earth in a rainstorm and got stuck out on the concrete, drying in the sun. It flicked about now and then, adding to this impression.

The exoodle looked frayed and torn, and Gregory couldn't help feeling sorry for it. The Grimbockle gave a sigh. "I is fixing everything I is able to here. I is having to head off to the mother end now."

"You mean to California?"

"Yes, Calee-for-nee-ya. There is no more moments left to spare. I is having to fix more than just this one threadling tonight."

"So exactly how many threads do you need to fix tonight?"

"Oodles. I is not even being able to count them all. Threads is breaking more these days than ever before."

"Why?" Gregory asked.

"Currents!" squawked the Grimbockle angrily.

Gregory wrinkled his nose in confusion. "Like sultanas?"

"No, no, none of your grapey sultanas. I is meaning currents like micro-waves and radio waves. Currents and waves is damaging more exoodles these days than anything else in the entire heavenly hemispheres."

"But how will you have time to fix so many tonight?"

The Grimbockle gave another sly grin, then pulled out a small, black disk from somewhere behind its back. This, it held proudly on the palm of its hand so that Gregory could plainly see it.

Before Gregory had a chance to ask, the Grimbockle pressed a tiny silver button on the side of the device, and the top popped open like a tiny little pocket watch. Gregory could see immediately that it was no ordinary pocket watch. In fact, there were so many parts moving inside of the device that it looked to Gregory like an entire factory had been compressed into the one small piece, with all its dials and lights and conveyer belts buzzing about.

"A dial scromple," said the Grimbockle reverently.

"Amazing!" said Gregory, leaning in for a better look. "What does it do?"

"A dial scromple is allowing us to play with days and times. You isn't thinking I is being able to get all my

workings done in hoo-man timings, is you?"

"I guess not," said Gregory.

"A dial scromple is not only slowing down days, but it is also allowing Bockles to be speeding up their comings and goings as well."

Gregory stared at the dial scromple, his eyebrows knitted tightly. "I wonder, is there any difference between slowing time down or speeding yourself up?"

The Grimbockle gave Gregory a careful scowl as it snapped the dial scromple shut. "You is full of rot and bother, you is. I is honestly starting to wonder if you is having anything inside your head but mashed po-taters."

Before Gregory even had a chance to be offended, the Grimbockle was producing another crystal bucket, this one with a silver-coloured liquid inside.

As with everything else so far, Gregory had no idea where the bucket had come from; the Grimbockle seemed to simply reach behind itself and pluck it straight out of the air.

"Okay, we is off," it said cheerfully. Then, before Gregory knew what was happening, it dipped another tiny brush straight in the tin and flicked a glob towards him with a practiced wrist. As it flew through the air, Gregory saw a silvery shimmer to the globule, which looked to him exactly like the fluid he had seen on the inside of his mother's thermometer.

For a second, he was terrified. This was because his mother had always said, "Gregory, if you ever break the thermometer glass and spill that silver liquid on yourself, it will burn through your body like acid."

Whether it was true or not, Gregory's mother had said it so many times that he now found himself petrified at the thought of thermometers breaking. And now, as the silvery globule soared towards his face, he wanted to run and had to remind himself that it wasn't the toxic thermometer fluid...at least, he hoped it wasn't.

As the liquid slapped across his face, Gregory thought it smelled like a punnet of freshly picked strawberries in the summer. Strangely enough, even though it was the smallest little bucket with the tiniest wee paintbrush, Gregory felt absolutely saturated by the liquid, like he had been caught in a sudden downpour of rain...in a straw-berry field.

Before he even had a chance to ask, a whoosh-ing noise, like a train whizzing past a platform, began to whistle through Gregory's ears. At the same time, he started to feel seasick—almost worse than the summer his parents had hired a house-boat. Shutting his eyes tight, he put his hands over his ears to block out the terrifying sound.

The sensation only lasted for maybe a second or two, and then it was over. Carefully, he moved his hands away from his ears and found the furi-ous whistling wind was gone as well.

Thank goodness for that! Gregory thought.

Opening his eyes, he immediately noticed two gigantic crystal paint tins sitting right beside him.

Hello, he thought. *The paint tins have gotten simply enormous...*

SILVER SHRINKER, said the huge label on one of the cans. CARROT JUICY, said the other.

Turning around slowly, Gregory found him-self looking at a gigantic set of lilac-y purple duck feet. He stared at these for a moment in shocked silence before finally allowing his gaze to travel up, up, up to where the hugely bulbous nose of the Grimbockle peered down at him in amusement.

"Oh-ho!" thundered the Grimbockle, rubbing its hands delightedly. "You is as tiny as a Trumpsicle now!"

Gregory started to ask what a Trumpsicle was, then thought better of it. Beside the Grimbockle stood the now hideously large cockroach. Puffed beyond reason to immense proportions, it stared down at Gregory with its great, ugly face, which was a terrible thing to behold.

Large as they were, Gregory felt a bit frightened. He found himself wondering what it was that Bockles and magical cockroach creatures ate.

"You've gotten bigger than me," he said with a slight catch in his throat.

"I is not growing," boomed the Grimbockle from high above Gregory's head. "You is shrinking."

Feeling his heart race, Gregory looked up and around. Sure enough, his bed was towering above them like Everest, so tall and vast, he couldn't see the top. Around them lay his dominos, scattered about like a small broken city, and on the wall shone his purple nightlight like a dim violet sun.

Once again, a rushing whistle filled the air. It sounded to Gregory like an overinflated balloon with the air inside escaping all at once through the small rubbery tail at its end. A second later, the Grimbockle stood before him at eye level, though, with its funny onion shaped head, it was still a little taller than Gregory.

The cockroach had shrunk less by comparison and looked monstrous to Gregory, like an ancient ankylosaur, sitting proudly with its broad armoured back.

The room loomed around them, a foreign landscape now. Judging by the building-sized domino beside him, Gregory guessed they were each about the size of a regular black garden ant.

"You've shrunk, too," said Gregory, stating the obvious.

"Of course, I is shrinking down! How else is we riding the Exoodle Expressway? Bockles is always adjusting our sizings to suit situations."

Tiny as they were, the exoodles seemed much larger but farther spread apart. They wound about the room and out through the windows and walls, looking like great shining roads and glittering highways.

Now that they were about the same size, Gregory couldn't help but notice how the Grimbockle's eyes kept darting back to the island-sized domino behind them.

"It's just a domino," said Gregory, wondering if the Grimbockle might be afraid.

"Dom-ee-no...dom-ee-no," said the Grimbockle, testing the word out. "What is, dom-ee-no? I is seeing it before, but I is never understanding it."

"Well, it's a sort of game humans play for fun. Not just one game, mind you—there are hundreds of ways to play. You can even make up new games by yourself!"

As Gregory spoke, he grew more and more excited. He loved his dominos, and people so rarely showed any interest in them at all.

"It used to be very popular, once upon a time, but I'm about the only person I know who plays with them these days."

He felt a little sad saying it. Yes, he felt very sad indeed. For what Gregory wanted most in the world was a friend to play dominos with, some-one to trade secrets and tactics with...someone to come up with strange new games and play with him all day long.

The Grimbockle was staring at the domino hungrily now.

"You can have one if you'd like," said Gregory, seeing the look in its eyes.

The Grimbockle looked taken aback. "Is you meaning it?"

"Help yourself!" said Gregory, pleased with the Grimbockle's interest in his beloved dominos.

Eyes aglow, the Grimbockle reached over for the crystal bucket (which had shrunk down with it) and flicked a generous lick of silver shrinker onto the domino. Seconds later, it sat in the palm of its hand, about the size of a slice of bread, with six dots on one half and two on the other.

"I is especially fond of hoo-man picoo-lee-ar-ities," said the Grimbockle, staring lovingly at the domino in its hand. "You is sure you is not minding?"

"Not at all!" said Gregory.

With a happy expression, the Grimbockle

tucked the domino, along with the crystal buckets of paint, back into the same space by its head from which Gregory had seen it pull them out.

One moment, the things were there in the Grimbockle's hand, and the next, they had quite literally vanished into thin air. It was very curious indeed, and Gregory had no idea how the Grimbockle had managed it. Some kind of magic, no doubt.

The Grimbockle flicked open the dial scromple once again and began to fiddle about with the various knobs and buttons. At his newly shrunken size, the dial scromple was about the size an ordinary apple would have been to Gregory at his full size. He could see little labels written around some of the buttons but found there was simply no way he could read the writing. In the end, he decided it was probably an entirely different language.

The Grimbockle fiddled with a few little toggles until it seemed satisfied, then pressed a small green button on the side. Giving a funny little beep, the dial scromple leapt to life, and the inner workings began to puff and whir.

The Grimbockle mounted its cockroach steed expertly, then offered Gregory a hand. "I has sped us up, and we is leaving now."

Gregory hesitated a second, staring at the Grimbockle's outstretched hand. The Grimbockle looked confused. "You is wanting to come, is you not?"

It was all happening so fast...Gregory wasn't sure he *should* be going on a strange little errand with a mysterious creature called the Grimbockle—in the middle of the night, no less. He also knew that, if he waited too long, he might never again have such a chance.

The moment he reached out his hand, the Grimbockle pulled him up onto the cockroach. Gregory sat firmly at the centre of its carapace. He expected to slide around on the oh-so-smooth surface but found, instead, that there was a deep groove, right where his bottom sat, which prevented this from happening. There was also a raised handle of sorts that he could hold onto to keep himself aboard this strange new mode of transport.

Even the sides of the carapace had been well

thought out, with little footholds into which his feet naturally slotted.

As soon as his feet slipped into place, their earnest steed was off, scuttling at a blinding pace straight towards the window.

"Hold on tigh-tilly little hoo-man!"

CHAPTER 6

Off to Calee-for-nee-ya

Gregory braced himself for impact as they bolted for the window, but they simply sailed through the glass as if it weren't there at all. For a moment, he thought they might be flying, but he quickly realised they were actually travelling atop a broad and particularly large exoodle thread. It was brilliant and bright with glittery speckles of light and seemed to flow like a great crystal river. Rather than winding around obstructions, the expressway and its passengers went straight through them, making Gregory cringe each time.

With their dial scromple–enhanced pace, they were making excellent time. Up they went over rooftops, then right by the local playground, following the Exoodle Expressway straight down Gregory's street.

As they sped along, Gregory couldn't help noticing a single light at the end of the neighbourhood. It started as just a tiny flicker in the distance, and then it was shining through a large window directly in front of him. He knew whose house it was right away; and for a sliver of a millisecond he caught sight of old Ethel in the window. She was hunched over the fireplace, staring sadly into the dying embers. Gregory thought he saw strange, twisting shadows wriggling above her head and decided to ask the Grimbockle about it later. Despite everything, Gregory couldn't help but feel sorry for old Ethel, looking so lost and forlorn. Before this moment, he had never given a thought to what her life might be like outside of her ritualistic ambush of his mole.

Soon, they were nearing his school, and as they soared over the grounds, Gregory poked out his tongue, blowing a raspberry for good measure.

They were gaining speed quite rapidly now, and the scenery began to flash by, like they were flicking through a life-sized stack of photographs.

They surged forward, picking up more and more speed. He caught sight of the exoodles here and there, floating like long glowworm filaments in the night sky. Now and then, he would spot an especially thick thread, like the one upon which they rode. He wondered what sorts of people had such thick, sturdy exoodles?

Exceptionally delightful people, Gregory supposed.

Occasionally, unattached threads would drift by, twisting and writhing in the air—like mosquito larvae in a stagnant pond. Once or twice, he spotted a cluster of them tangled together messily like tumbleweeds.

Soon, they were shooting out past the town centre, then flying over some hills, and finally springing forward across the ocean. Once they were there, the cockroach increased its speed. Faster and faster they flew, until Gregory could see only a blur of black all around him and the expressway glowing beneath them like a great, tangible moonbeam. It was a peculiar sensation, for somehow, Gregory felt as though he was no longer moving at all. Only the sound of the wind whistling past his ears and the occasional splotches of light, which he assumed must be ships out on the dark, endless sea, reminded him he was travelling.

The wind was so loud that Gregory didn't even bother trying to talk to the Grimbockle. He didn't really feel like talking much, anyway, for he was quite enjoying this magical midnight ride across the ocean, even if he couldn't see much at the moment.

Despite his initial misgivings about the peculiar cockroach transport, Gregory decided it was a lovely ride indeed. With its six nimble legs, the cockroach seemed to glide across the Exoodle

Expressway like a stick of butter in a frypan, with no jolts or jarring of any kind. Not like the time Gregory had gone horse-riding with his family. That had been a nightmare...and he'd had such high expectations, too. After all, people adored horses, wrote stories about them, painted pictures of them—so it seemed obvious to Gregory that his first experience with such a noble beast would be simply magnificent. He had pictured himself swinging atop his valiant mount and galloping through flowering hills of honeysuckle. Yet, when he'd finally clambered upon the fat old mare with mud-flecked flanks, it had broken off into a mad, bolting gallop, and poor Gregory had been bounced about like a sack of potatoes. And if that wasn't bad enough, the sour old creature had thrown him off in the end, right into a sloppy puddle of mud. Gregory hadn't been able to sit down comfortably for at least a week after that. Needless to say, he'd hated horses ever since.

Feeling suddenly grateful, Gregory gave the cockroach a gentle pat on its back, thanking it for such a smooth, steady ride.

Gregory noticed they were gradually slowing

down. He could tell this by the wind, which was no longer roaring so loudly in his ears. Ahead of them, a great, cliffy coastline was glistening like a silver serpent in the moonlight, and soon they were gliding over the sandy beach. They sailed past gently swaying palm trees, over an enormous infinity pool, and finally straight through the window of an exceptionally plush-looking hotel room.

They skidded to a halt right beside a telephone sitting on a short, wooden table. It was such an abrupt stop that Gregory flew off the back of the cockroach, tumbled off the table, and fell straight towards the floor. At his current size, the fall from the table to the floor was like jumping straight off a twelve-story building.

I'm dead, he thought as the ground rushed up to meet him. *What a short life that was.*

He closed his eyes and braced himself for the impact—then opened them five seconds later to find that (most peculiarly) he was still alive. You see, Gregory weighed almost nothing at all now, and much like an ant falling from the top of a picnic table, or a leaf fluttering down from its tree, he was totally intact and not damaged in the slightest.

On top of this, he'd landed on the soft corner of a ridiculously plush bed covering, which was hanging down from a king-sized four-poster bed. The bed itself was one of those exotic things with dozens of cushions and billowing silk curtains draped around it.

Though unhurt, Gregory was still in shock and lay sprawled exactly as he'd landed, upside down on a fold of fabric, breathing heavily with a slight rattling wheeze.

The Grimbockle (who had come down from the table on the cockroach) alighted beside him expertly, looking rather smug. "I is telling you to hold on tigh-tilly, is I not?" It gave a hearty chuckle at Gregory's expense.

Gregory drew a deep, shaky breath, then tried to right himself by wriggling his arms and kicking out his legs like a chicken in a sand bath. After a good twenty seconds of wriggling and kicking, he was finally the right way up and standing on two feet again.

Now that he was upright, he immediately

noticed the loud snoring coming from the top of the bed. At their tiny size, it was like the loudest thunder, filling Gregory's ears and rattling his body to the bones. It was a horrendous sound, and Gregory wondered how anyone could sleep through that sort of racket.

Meanwhile, the Grimbockle was pulling out a bucket Gregory hadn't seen before. He stared at the new bucket suspiciously. This one, like the two others, was made of the same crystal clear material he could see straight through, but inside was a lovely gold liquid with a soft, metallic glow—quite beautiful to look at.

"What is it?" said Gregory, awestruck.

"We is much too tiny for being useful now, so I is making us just the tinkiest wink bigger with some Golden Grower."

They didn't bother whispering, for at their current size, the people sleeping in the bed above were as likely to hear them as one would be to hear termites nibbling away at a house.

Now that he was the same size as the Grimbockle, Gregory could easily read the label on the side of the bucket. GOLDEN GROWER, it declared, exactly as the Grimbockle had said.

"What's it made of?" asked Gregory, suddenly feeling a little nervous.

"Gold!" sang the Grimbockle ecstatically. "Everyone is knowing silver is shrinking things, squiddly small, and gold is growing them, bonny and bold!"

Not everyone, Gregory thought.

Of the three so far, Golden Grower was without a doubt Gregory's favourite. To begin with, it felt very smooth and light when the Grimbockle began painting him with it, and it had the fresh scent of a recently watered rose garden.

The process of growing was also much less offensive than the process of shrinking, but Gregory supposed this had something to do with the fact that they had only grown a little bit. They were now both very close to the size the Grimbockle had been when Gregory had first met him, and it was quite a delightful size to be. Gregory felt quick and nimble as if his arms and legs were filled with springs and rubber.

The Grimbockle seemed preoccupied, fiddling with the dial scromple.

"What now?" said Gregory, watching suspiciously as the Grimbockle tinkered. He was still feeling a bit put out by the whole falling incident and hadn't quite forgiven the Grimbockle for laughing at him.

"Now, we is slowing things down," said the Grimbockle. "We is slowing things down so we is having oodles of time for exoodles."

As he watched the Grimbockle fiddle with all the dials and knobs, Gregory suddenly had a thought that made his heart beat a little bit faster. "I wonder," he said carefully. "If you have the dial scromple, couldn't you just go back in time and fix things any time you pleased?" For Gregory had begun to wonder if the dial scromple might actually be a time machine.

The Grimbockle looked quite ruffled at the question. "You is speaking hogs and washes you is! Dial scromples is only being able to slow down time or speed it up. They is not actually being able to go *back* in time. Time that is passing is already passed. We is never being able to return to it." The Grimbockle gave a little huff and shook its head. "No. No one is ever going *back* in time.

I is only slowing down the minutes so they is not ticking away so fast."

"I see," said Gregory, disappointed.

Like most everyone in the world, there were things Gregory would have dearly liked to go back and change. For instance, if he'd never ridden that wretched horse, he'd never have been bucked off. And if he'd never been bucked off, his family wouldn't have had another reason to laugh at and mock him. He knew he was still holding a grudge over that and wondered if, perhaps, such things were to blame for the sorry state of his family exoodles.

"Say," said Gregory, suddenly alarmed, "will the whole world slow down when you use the dial scromple?"

"It is exactly as you is saying."

"But then, I mean...is it fair to slow the whole world down and then suddenly spring it forward as you please?"

"Is you not always feeling like this anyway? Time is being very mysterious. It is not always behaving how hoo-mans is expecting it to. They is feeling it is slowing down, but they is not understanding why. Hoo-mans, after all, is not understanding time as Bockles is understanding time. Bockles is playing with time as hoo-mans is playing with yo-yos and baskety-balls."

Gregory was silent, thinking to himself that the Grimbockle had a point. He was always feeling that time had a curious way of speeding up and slowing down.

It seemed to go very fast when he was having fun and exceptionally slow on rainy days, or when he was at school. Still, it was rather a lot to take in, and Gregory's head was starting to feel like it had been stuffed full of candy fluff.

"But how does it all work?" he finally managed to say. "Slowing down time and all?"

"Ah! Now we is getting deep and dark as Davey Jones-es locker! Even if I is somehow explaining it to you, you is not being able to see it. Hoo-mans is only seeing the world in 2 and 3Ds, after all. Bockles is seeing the world in up to *12* at least!"

"Twelve! Whatever is 12D?"

"Like I is saying, even if I is trying to explain it to you, your head will be exploding off your neck like a moon rocket. Even if you *is* somehow understanding it, you is still never being able to see it with those little twinklers."

At the mention of eyes, Gregory looked again at the Grimbockle's. At least five times larger than his own, they bulged out of its head, like black crystal orbs. If he stared at them long enough, he felt he could see all kinds of things spinning around inside them, like each was its own little solar system. Yes, he supposed if he had such eyes, he would be able to see a world of wonderful things.

CHAPTER 7

The Note

The Grimbockle had grown quiet now. Its face wore a grim expression as it waddled over and picked up the frayed line of an exoodle, which led up onto the bed and out of Gregory's sight. With the delicate webbings between its fingers, the Grimbockle's hand looked made for the task and seemed to attract the exoodles rather than repel them the way Gregory's hand had.

"This is even worse than I is anticipating. This hoo-man is badly needing to call her Tommy."

"So, Tommy's her son?"

"Yes. I is already telling you all about him," said the Grimbockle impatiently.

"But how do you know his name?" asked Gregory.

"The exoodle is telling me. This mumsie is forgetting for weeks to call her Tommy, and now he is so dumpy and down, he is damaging the exoodle himself."

"How horrid! Why would anyone do such a thing?"

"He is not knowing he is doing it. He is just feeling frightfully cross and sad. He is thinking his mumsie is not loving him, and these thoughts is damaging exoodles like rain is damaging ponds."

"How on earth could rain damage ponds?"

The Grimbockle gave a brusque sigh and looked over at Gregory with disapproval.

"It is pouring down out the sky, is it not?"

"Yes," said Gregory, not certain where the Grimbockle was headed.

"It is falling straight into ponds, but it is also pouring everywhere on the earth's crusty coating, is it not?"

Gregory could think of absolutely nothing to say to this, so he remained quiet while the Grimbockle continued.

"All these drops is running together—earth, sea, and sky—and they is running and running until, finally, they is filling up in rivers, lakes, and ponds! Lakes is very big, and rivers is all eventually running back to sea. But ponds is being changed for life, is they not?"

Gregory wasn't quite convinced by the Grimbockle's logic, and yet its bizarre explanations always made sense, somehow.

The image of angry flood waters was something Gregory knew well. The river just outside the town where he lived was constantly flooding. One day, the floods had reached the town. He could still remember the roiling, churning water sucking everything into it, changing some of the landscape forever and, yes, probably changing plenty of the ponds as well.

"What can we do?" he said, looking sadly at the ripped and ragged exoodle thread.

The Grimbockle shook its head, then gently lay the exoodle down.

"I is probably needing reinforcements for this kind of job. But first, we is seeing if it is possible to be fixing things from the other side."

"Tommy's side?" Gregory asked.

"Yes. Fixing things from Tommy's side is what I is trying next."

A curious expression crossed Gregory's face. "What about his father?" he asked, pointing to the man sleeping beside Tommy's mother.

"I is only realising recently that his father force is not here," said the Grimbockle sheepishly. "This is his step-daddles, and they is not forming any exoodles between them yet. We is needing to do something before it is getting too late. The situation is rising higher and higher every second."

The Grimbockle began to fish about in the air behind it, looking for the Silver Shrinker. Gregory stood perfectly still, a thousand thoughts boiling in his head all at once. He felt certain he should try to do something to help. He couldn't stand knowing that Tommy was out there, feeling so sad, he was damaging his own exoodles.

What can I do? he wondered.

The Grimbockle stood before him brandishing the silver-dipped paintbrush and swishing a bit on itself. "We is leaving now, little hoo-man."

"Wait a minute," said Gregory, stopping the Grimbockle mid-swish.

Turning around, he ran back to where he had first fallen, then nimbly clambered straight up the bed covering and onto the top of the bed.

The heavy breathing of Tommy's mother and stepfather was much louder now that he was closer to it. Gregory thought it sounded like two enormous trucks rumbling and roaring down the highway.

As quickly as he could, he made his way forward across the top of the bed. This was not as easy as he'd first imagined it would be, for it was a very thick blanket, folded here and there in great mountains and deep valleys of fabric. In many places the soft padding of the blanket gave way beneath him, and in these places, he wound up wading through walls of feathery softness like deep drifts of snow. Once he had puffed his way up one particularly high spot, he was able to see across to the table and spied exactly what he was hoping to. He knew most fancy hotels supplied a notepad and pen at the bedside, and Gregory had been counting on both of them being there.

Wiping his brow, he continued his journey toward the table.

Suddenly, Tommy's stepfather began to roll over in his sleep. The blankets shifted under Gregory's feet, causing him to lose his balance and fall flat on his back. He had only seconds to gawk up in horror at the tsunami-sized backside towering over him before it rolled directly on top of him.

It was dark and stuffy under the blankets. At first, Gregory thought he couldn't move at all, but his tiny size saved him once again. Quickly, he wriggled towards the direction he hoped was out and found himself emerging from the sheets, breathing the fresh, free air. Shaken, Gregory lay sprawled on the blanket, gasping. Eventually, he composed himself and set back out towards the table, this time with greater care.

Gregory picked up the pen, which was about the size of the drainpipe hanging off his house. Being plastic, it was very light, so he was still able to manage it at his tiny size.

He knew he didn't have a lot of time. Already, he could see the Grimbockle down on the ground, fiddling impatiently with the dial scromple and pacing back and forth. He had to think quickly. He had to write the perfect words.

Though the pen was light, Gregory still had to use both hands to hold it steady. Fortunately, it was a black gel pen with nice bold ink. This made it a little easier for him as he moved the pen along awkwardly.

Making as little sound as possible, Gregory tore the note from the pad and moved quietly off the table. He crept along the pathway that existed between the pillow and the headboard, working his way toward the middle of the bed. Soon, he found himself face-to-face with Tommy's mother.

While Gregory thought she had a relatively kind face, he did wonder what might make a person worry so hard that they even looked worried in their sleep. Until this very moment, Gregory had been feeling rather annoyed with Tommy's mother. After all, swimming with sea otters didn't seem like a good enough reason to be away from Tommy for so many weeks. Yet now, as he watched her trying to sleep with all those lines of worry, he couldn't help but feel sorry for her as well.

He stared at the frayed exoodle, coming right from the place above her heart. It was so thick, Gregory thought it must have been strong once. But now, it was weathered and frayed like the tattered rope on the end of a very old anchor.

Gregory read the note he'd written one more time. Because of the size of the pen, the lettering looked like the clumsy writing of a five-year-old. He hoped Tommy's mother would be able to read it.

You must call Tommy now and tell him how very special he is. That he is the most wonderful boy in the world and that you love him more than anything. You must go home to him soon!

Gregory had underlined "soon!" twice for good measure. He knew if *he'd* found such a note, he would most certainly call, no matter what time it was. He knew he needed to place the note where Tommy's mother was sure to see it. This was, perhaps, the most dangerous part of his mission, for one wrong move and he might wake her up. Using painstaking care, he lowered the note, ever so gently, until it came to rest in her hand. He did this so slowly, and so carefully, that even if Tommy's mother had been awake, it is unlikely she would have noticed.

When the mission was complete, Gregory made his way back through the pillow tunnel and along the edge of the mattress, to the foot of the bed, where he joyfully slid down the covering, as though it were a giant slide. He stood before the Grimbockle, unable to keep the grin off his face. The Grimbockle narrowed its eyes and regarded Gregory suspiciously.

"What is you doing up there little hoo-man?"

"Tinkering," said Gregory, feeling pleased.

The Grimbockle watched him a little while longer before finally giving a little huff and saying under its breath, "I is never fully understanding hoo-mans and their picoo-lee-arities."

CHAPTER 8

Dark Exoodles

Once they had shrunk back down to their former sizes, it was off again on the Exoodle Expressway. As they flew across the ocean at a blinding pace, Gregory wondered where they were headed. It could be anywhere, he supposed—Africa, China, or perhaps that funny little country, New Zealand.

Gregory had heard all about New Zealand from his best friend, Clarence, who had moved there with his family. According to Clarence, there were all kinds of wonderful things in New Zealand... volcanos, hot springs, and funny flightless birds called Kiwis. These, he said, looked like giant kiwifruits on stilts with long straws for beaks.

Remembering this made Gregory miss his friend terribly. He thought about asking the Grimbockle if they could stop off in New Zealand, but then he thought better of it. Despite the distance and time, his exoodle for Clarence was stronger than ever, and as much as he would have liked to see his friend, Gregory knew the situation with Tommy was growing desperate. Besides, any words he said were sure to be sucked out into the roaring wind anyway.

They seemed to be travelling faster this time, for Gregory could already see land approaching. Before he knew it, they were gliding through a small city, then crossing a patchwork of suburbs, and finally flying straight through another closed window.

This time, the cockroach steed appeared to misjudge its landing, and all three of them tumbled over together onto a plush, maroon rug. Gregory could only tell what colour the rug was because a light was still on in the room. When he looked up at the desk, he could also see why the cockroach had landed so badly, for there, just in the place they had attempted to land, was a sleeping boy with his head resting on the desktop. Gregory knew it must be Tommy.

The Grimbockle looked up at the sleeping Tommy. "Oh dear! Oh dear! This is a very tricky situation indeed!"

"What should we do?" said Gregory.

The Grimbockle thought for a moment and then began fishing about for something in the air beside its head. For the first time, Gregory was paying attention at just the right moment, as the fabric of the universe seemed to become magically tangible at the Grimbockle's touch. He simply reached in and opened it up as casually as one might open a closet door in the morning.

For a few moments, Gregory was able to see the space inside. It looked about the size of a large pantry; only it wasn't stocked with food at all. The shelves were bursting with all kinds of things Gregory couldn't even begin to guess at: whirling wheels and twirling gears, hundreds of tiny vials, and jars filled with things that were moving all by themselves.

Buckets, exactly like the ones Gregory had

already seen, lined the bottom row of the shelf. He soon spotted the labels of the three he knew: GOLDEN GROWER, SILVER SHRINKER, and CARROT JUICY. There were other labels with even more peculiar names: RUBBER STRETCHY, DIAMOND SKIN SHIELD, and FURRY FEATHER FLUFF.

All of the buckets were made from the same crystal clear material, so Gregory could see the colours of the liquid inside, but one bucket wasn't filled with liquid at all. It had a curious label: HOOMAN THINGS.

When Gregory looked a little closer, he saw the bucket was packed to the brim with bits and pieces of this and that. Poking proudly out the top was the domino he'd given the Grimbockle. Gregory smiled at this, feeling certain he'd made a new friend.

The Grimbockle held a bucket, which looked empty at first glance, but as Gregory stared at it longer, he was sure he saw something *moving* inside it.

As the fluid inside began to take shape, it appeared to be rather like glue, or the sticky sort of sap that drips out of a tree. But it wasn't the colour of either. It was radiantly transparent, sparkling like diamonds in the sun, and each time he looked at it, the colour changed. Gregory thought it was extraordinary.

"Exoodle Juice!" said the Grimbockle, as if sensing the question.

"That's terrible!" cried Gregory, moving away from the bucket so quickly he almost knocked the Grimbockle over. "You can't juice exoodles!"

"Poppycock!" said the Grimbockle when it regained its balance. "Exoodles is only being juiced from old and unused threads, and they is much preferring to be made useful rather than left on their lonesome."

"But it seems so cruel to tear them to shreds."

"Yes, they is getting torn to shreds, but they is not minding it at all. Exoodles is enjoying being juiced the way hoo-mans is enjoying a trip to the fair and riding on roly-coasters."

"I see," said Gregory, feeling relieved. "But, what are we going to do with exoodle juice anyway?"

"Ordinary hoo-mans is not seeing exoodles, is they?"

"No..."

"Now, they is not seeing us either!"

With a quick dip and a flick of the wrist, the Grimbockle splotched the liquid all over Gregory and then did the same thing to the cockroach and to itself. When the droplets hit Gregory, they didn't stay in one place but instead spread out all over until a thin coating covered his entire body.

As he stood beside the Grimbockle, he saw then that they were both translucent.

"Say, why didn't you paint yourself with this earlier?" asked Gregory. "I wouldn't have spotted you at all if you had."

The Grimbockle lifted its nose a little, then looked away. "We is not asking questions about things that is already passing away from us."

It jumped back onto the cockroach and waited there for Gregory, quiet and aloof.

Once Gregory had clambered up onto the

cockroach's back, they shot up the leg of the desk, landed on the tabletop, then dismounted quietly on the surface where they were supposed to have landed in the first place.

Once the Grimbockle had alighted, it gave the cockroach a good-natured rub behind its antenna and spoke softly to it.

"You is always doing a good job, you is. We is not worrying at all about one or two bumpy landings."

The cockroach arched and reared against the Grimbockle like a cat, clearly enjoying the rub.

Giving the beast a final pat, the Grimbockle moved slowly over to Tommy.

At their minuscule size, the shape of the boy sleeping before them was like a small mountain range.

Slouched over the tabletop, Tommy had rested his head on one of his arms. The other was stretched out above him, fingers loosely wound around the mobile phone he had fallen asleep clutching.

Gregory could see the exoodle thread they'd been tracking all night, sticking straight out of Tommy's back. He could clearly see it was more damaged on

Tommy's end. There were ragged chunks hanging off the sides and some kind of fluid seeping from its core and dripping out onto the table.

The Grimbockle let out a deep, heavy breath.

"Even I is not knowing what to do now. I is rarely seeing exoodles this damaged and still attached. Even if we is bringing in backup, I is not sure we is able to be fixing it. But it is oh-so dangerous for it to still be attached in this sorry state! Oh-so dangerous indeed!"

Gregory was about to ask why it was so dangerous when something in Tommy's hair caught his attention.

At first glance, it looked just like any other curly brown hair. Yet, as he looked closer, Gregory saw that it wasn't sitting still the way hair should. Instead, it was wriggling and writhing about.

Right when he thought he'd better mention it to the Grimbockle, dozens of dark threads came bursting out of Tommy's hair, like black, squirming worms. Several shot straight at Gregory. As they came towards him, the air around them became stale and darker, and Gregory felt a deep sense of dread.

He was certain he was about to be knocked dead or gobbled up whole, but the Grimbockle intervened by tipping an entire bucket of something that smelled very much like cherry pie and violets right on the top of Gregory's head.

The creatures froze, only millimetres from Gregory's face. They had no eyes or even faces, only huge, gaping mouths with beastly smelling breath and hundreds of rows of teeth leading all the way down into their throats.

They moved around in the air as if searching for Gregory, but eventually gave up and returned to their nest in Tommy's hair.

"What were those?" said Gregory, once he could speak again.

The Grimbockle's face had grown dark.

"Those is dark exoodles," it said bitterly, glaring at the top of Tommy's head. "If dark exoodles is forming, we is in dire straits indeed. I is not often seeing dark exoodles forming on so young a hoo-man."

Gregory was still trembling from the shock.

"But why were they coming for me?"

"Dark exoodles is an oh-so pesty infestation of paree-sites. They is growing and thriving on one head, and then they is spreading like itchy-snitchy rashes! They is always trying to latch onto anyone or anything they is able to, and they is often succeeding."

Though they were indoors, Gregory could feel a chill running down his neck and taking up residence deep in his spine.

The Grimbockle shook its head back and forth, seeming flustered.

"When dark exoodles is finding good threads that is becoming rough and ragged, they is latching on with their million little tooths-es, and they is not letting go! Dark exoodles is not starting new and fresh-fangled like healthy ones is. They is multiplying in number when they is grabbing on and passing over from one sadly hoo-man to the next. Once they is taking firm hold of a hoo-man, all the other hoo-man's threads is suffering."

"Well, thank you for saving me, then," Gregory said with a nervous chuckle. "What was it you poured over me anyway?"

The Grimbockle showed him the empty bucket so Gregory could read the label.

ESSENCE OF LOVE, it said.

"Love is the only thing that is stopping dark exoodles from attacking vul-neer-able hoo-mans."

Inside the bucket, Gregory could still see traces of the rich, red fluid. Strangely, there was none of it left on Gregory. He shouldn't have been surprised, though, for he knew the Grimbockle's buckets of paint were all mysterious and magical.

"What should we do about Tommy?" Gregory asked with concern.

"We is not able to do anything now. Once dark exoodles is attached, we is not able to do anything much at all. Sometimes, they is disappearing by themselves, but usually, they is multiplying and spreading over to other hoo-mans."

"So, we can't get rid of them?" said Gregory, aghast.

"Bockles is not yet knowing how."

"What about Essence of Love?"

"Essence of Love is being oh-so difficult to be extracting in large amounts. Even if we is having enough, painting hoo-mans is not working to get rid of them when dark exoodles is already being attached."

As Gregory thought about this, he felt even sorrier for Tommy. He couldn't imagine having such terribly wretched things living in his hair.

Suddenly, the phone in Tommy's hand lit up and began buzzing and ringing wildly. The Grimbockle squeaked in horror and clutched at its heart. "Oh, my wriggling rump! Oh, my sweet liver dandies!"

The cockroach steed seemed shell-shocked as well and scuttled madly left and right, waiting for orders from its master. The phone continued buzzing, and Tommy started to stir, but the Grimbockle stood, frozen stiff with fear.

"Hey!" whispered Gregory, giving the Grimbockle a shake.

But there was no response. The Grimbockle had fainted again.

Gregory panicked, not sure what to do. The Essence of Love, which was still wafting through the air, seemed to have reversed the effect of the Exoodle Juice, and they were no longer invisible.

Frantically, Gregory grabbed onto one of the Grimbockle's webbed hands and pulled them both onto the cockroach's back. He reached for the creature's antennae the way he had seen the Grimbockle do. With a gentle nudge, Gregory was able to quickly guide the cockroach into the folds of some wadded up paper, which sat on the desktop.

Tommy stirred, and Gregory saw him glance sleepily at the paper they had just disappeared into. Just as he thought he'd been spotted, Gregory saw Tommy shift his focus to the phone, which was still ringing wildly in his hand.

Tommy sat watching the phone ring. He didn't seem to want to pick it up. Before Gregory had a chance to wonder why, he noticed the dark exoodles stirring in Tommy's hair once again. He desperately wished the Grimbockle hadn't fainted. He had no idea what to do.

Finally, Tommy clicked a button and put the phone to his ear, but he didn't say anything.

In the stillness of the evening, Gregory found he was able to hear every word from the person on the other line.

"Tommy!" came the frantic voice. "Tommy, is everything all right?"

"What do you mean? I'm fine," he finally said, his voice flat.

"Oh!" said the other voice. "I'm so relieved!"

"Well, what did you expect?" he muttered under his breath.

The dark exoodles rose up out of Tommy's hair now and began writhing above his head, seeming aggravated by the conversation. Tommy looked bored and began fiddling with the fastener at the back of the watch he was wearing, putting it on and taking it off...over and over again.

"I was worried about you," said the woman, who Gregory knew must be Tommy's mother.

"Oh, how sweet," said Tommy with a dry, coarse laugh, not fitting for a boy at all. "I didn't realise you still cared enough to worry."

"What are you saying? Of course I worry," came his mother's voice. "I am your mother, after all."

As soon as she said, "I am your mother," something strange happened. The exoodle that hung limp and torn from Tommy's back, seemed to be trying to breathe, erratically swelling and collapsing again.

Gregory turned toward the Grimbockle, expecting to see it still lying unconscious, but was surprised to find its big, black eyes glued to Tommy's exoodle as well. Gregory started to whisper something to the Grimbockle, but it put its hand up and shook its head, so he remained silent. Like spectators, they observed Tommy anxiously.

Tommy picked up his watch and stared at it numbly. Suddenly, his eyes widened, and he drew it up closer to his face. Giving it a tap, he put it to his ear, as if checking to see if it was still working, then threw it down and looked at his phone instead.

"It's 1:30 in the morning," he said to his mother.

"Yes, I know," she answered quietly.

"Why would you call in the middle of the night?"

"Like I said, I was worried," she began apologetically. "I found a note...and, well...I realised I hadn't called you in a while and...anyway, I wanted to hear your voice. Tommy, I know I haven't always been a good mother...."

Her voice trailed off for a moment like she'd lost the courage to finish her sentence. Finally, she seemed to find her thoughts again.

"Things are going to be different now. I just want you to know that."

When Tommy spoke, it was in a small voice. "Different...how?"

The line went quiet for a moment.

"Well, I can promise you one thing. I won't ever let you forget how special you are. I love you—more than anything."

Tommy closed his eyes, and Gregory saw a tear push out from the corner of one of them.

Tommy quickly wiped the tear away and unconsciously pressed his lips firmly into a pout.

"Will you be coming home then?" he asked, a tiny bit of hope stealing into his voice.

Gregory and the Grimbockle seemed as anxious for the answer as Tommy must have been.

"Yes, Tommy. I'll book a flight first thing in the morning."

Gregory and the Grimbockle looked at each other and smiled. When they turned back to Tommy, they noticed the dark exoodles behaving strangely. Their movements were sluggish, and they looked wilted, weak, and altogether much less fierce.

The exoodle coming from Tommy's back was still pulsing slowly, but the pulses were becoming steadier, like the rhythm of a fragile heart.

The Grimbockle tapped Gregory urgently and pointed to the end of the exoodle that was coming in from the window. Something was flooding into it, and its faded colour was changing to a warm, comforting pink. Gregory thought it looked like a long straw filling up with fresh strawberry milk. Quickly, it made its way through the exoodle and all the way up to Tommy.

Gregory held his breath.

He could see the blood-red fluid shooting through the exoodle, filling the room with the smell of fresh cherry pie and violets.

"*Real* love," said the Grimbockle in reverent shock, confirming Gregory's suspicion.

By now, the phone conversation had finished, but Tommy was still holding onto the phone and staring at it hard. Just then, a tear dropped onto the desktop, then another and another. A steady flow of love pumped through the exoodle, right into Tommy's back, sending gentle waves of pink all the way through his body.

Tommy fiddled with his phone for a moment, then laid it down on the desktop. He stood up, wiped his eyes, and made his way over to his bed. Almost as soon as he crawled under the covers, Tommy was snoring.

Gregory wondered how he could sleep with so much love pumping through his body, but then he thought, perhaps, that was precisely why he could.

As soon as it heard the snoring, the Grimbockle sprinted over to the place Tommy had been only moments before. It painted itself slightly larger as it went.

There, in the exact spot Tommy's head had been resting, lay the dark exoodles...dying. Wriggling and writhing, they gnashed their hundreds of teeth and finally, with a little puff, disappeared entirely.

The Grimbockle stared at the empty spot as if it couldn't believe its eyes.

"What *is* you doing back in Calee-for-nee-ya, Gregor-ee?" it said, using Gregory's name for the first time.

"Oh, not much," said Gregory, blushing a little, and wondering himself how one small message could accomplish such a big and beautiful thing.

When they stepped over Tommy's phone on their way back to the cockroach steed, the screen lit up. There, glowing in front of them were the words Tommy had typed...I LOVE YOU, MUM.

CHAPTER 9

Bocklia

The Grimbockle stared hard at Gregory as if he had suddenly sprouted horns and an enormous bushy tail.

"It was just a little note," said Gregory, trying to explain.

"A note! What sort of mind-sniggling note is slaying dark exoodles and summoning love? These two eyes of mine is never seeing such things in any of their years!" The Grimbockle narrowed its eyes a little and said, "Is you having some kind of magic powers you is not telling us about?"

"No!" said Gregory, feeling alarmed. "All I did was write a short note telling Tommy's mother she had to call him...that she had to get home to Tommy."

The Grimbockle looked unconvinced. But before either of them had a chance to continue the conversation, a strange beeping sound came from the Grimbockle.

Looking surprised, the Grimbockle slipped its hand into a pocket at its side—a pocket that seemed to be part of the Grimbockle's body. Fishing around for a while, it finally pulled out a square, flashing object.

"I is being paged," said the Grimbockle, looking ill.

"Paged?"

"My home bases is calling us back."

"You mean, back to my mole?"

"I is telling you already, Gregor-ee. Bockles is using hoo-man moles like holiday houses—temper-air-rilly, and only when we is having rumbling bumbling amounts of work to be doing."

"So where are you going now?" Gregory asked.

"Not me...*we* is being summoned."

Right at that moment, the Grimbockle's pager sent out a red laser beam. It spun around them both, like the large glowing hand of a clock. Faster and faster it spun in every direction, putting Gregory and the Grimbockle right in the centre of a small red sphere of light.

Inside the light bubble, everything became blurred, and the air around them started to shake.

"Whaaat's haaappening?" asked Gregory.

The Grimbockle never answered, but Gregory saw fear in its large, black eyes. There was a loud pop, then a mad rushing sensation, which made Gregory feel as if all of his limbs were being pulled to bits. This sensation lasted only a second or two before he found they were standing on solid ground once again.

Now that the circle of red had receded, Gregory could see they were no longer in Tommy's room, and, in fact, didn't seem to be on Earth at all. It was bright and sunny where he was, but the light was coming from a sky quite different from the one on Earth. It was a mixture of green and purple with the two colours blending into one another. The source of the light was three pink suns—two were quite small, and one was absolutely enormous.

The greenish-grey landscape was splashed with magenta and orange, and everything was cast with a gentle pink glow from the three bright suns. The trees (if you could call them that) were many different colours, and their leaves looked fluffy and soft, like mountains of feathery down. They stood tall in the sky like pines but weeping like willows. Creatures, like enormous dragonflies, glided amongst them— quiet, ethereal giants of the air.

Having missed out on the Grimbockle's most recent painting, Gregory was still very small, so to him, the whole place looked even wilder than if he had been his normal size. Then again, he wasn't sure what a normal size was in this place. Suddenly feeling afraid, he looked for the Grimbockle but didn't see him.

While Gregory was deciding what to do, he heard a sound coming from the unusual world around him.

"G...eee!"

Gregory's eyes grew wide with wonder...and fear.

"G...Eeee! G...Eeee!"

Whatever it was, it was getting closer.

"Gre...Reee! Gre...Reee!"

Gregory looked for a place to hide, just in case, but then he recognised the voice. It was the Grimbockle calling to him.

"Gregor-ee! Gregor-ee!"

"Here! I'm here!" Gregory yelled as loudly as he could. He kept yelling, until the Grimbockle finally burst out from the undergrowth and stood puffing and heaving before him, as if it had just finished running a marathon.

"Gregor-ee," it finally managed, "Is you okay?"

"I think so," he answered. "What happened? Where are we?"

"We is in the Brumbly Jungle in Bocklia," said the Grimbockle. "Bocklia is where Bockles is coming from."

"Oh!" said Gregory relieved. "So, you've brought us to your home. Why didn't you say so in the first place?"

The Grimbockle looked at Gregory, shaking its head. "No, Gregor-ee. I is not bringing us here. *They* is bringing us. They is overriding my transporter pager, and they is zooming us here through space and time. But we is being scattered all over the Brumbly, because they is trying to bring two of us at once. Two at once is not being the usual way."

"Oh," said Gregory, feeling uneasy again.

They had been so busy talking, neither had noticed the unnatural stillness settling in around them. The Jungle had grown quiet, and the dragonfly birds had vanished. They didn't see the shadows moving softly through the trees until they were already surrounded.

"We be the royal Guardbockles! And we be taking you to the Grandbockle!" cried one of the creatures in the circle around them.

The Guardbockles that stood before them had silver bands around their heads and wore armour that seemed to be made from pieces of the jungle. They had stern expressions on their faces, which might have made them look quite fierce if it hadn't been for the tall pink feathers that stood up from the fronts of their headbands. They looked so out of place, Gregory felt inclined to laugh, but he resisted.

"My friends," said the Grimbockle nervously, "what is being the problem here?"

"You be coming with us," said one of the Guardbockles in a high, squeaking voice.

At the sound of the Guardbockle's shrill, silly voice, all the laughter Gregory had been holding in came bursting out. Before he knew it, he was doubled over, laughing so hard his body was shaking and tears were running like rivers down his face.

"Gregor-ee," the Grimbockle said, sounding horrified.

Gregory knew he shouldn't be laughing, given their current predicament, but now that he'd started, he just couldn't stop.

The Guardbockles were staring at him fiercely when one of them said, "What be wrong with zis hoo-man, Grimbockle?"

"I is not sure," said the Grimbockle, looking at Gregory worriedly. "I is never seeing him doing this."

"Perhaps you be breaking it on the way over here. If zis is so, you be making zings easy for us. But we be leaving zis for the Grandbockle to be deciding."

Their captors positioned them so they were right in the middle of the group and set off through the Brumbly Jungle.

The Grimbockle picked up Gregory, who was still tiny, and placed him inside its shirt pocket where he could speak to him.

"Who is the Grandbockle?" asked Gregory, finally serious again.

The Grimbockle looked forlorn. "The Grandbockle is to Bockles as kings-es and queens-es is to hoo-mans. If the Grandbockle is summoning us, we is in oh-so deep waters indeed."

"What be you two whispering about?" screeched one of the Guardbockles, nearly knocking Gregory off the Grimbockle's shoulder. "We be having silence from you now."

CHAPTER 10

The Grandbockle

As they walked through the Brumbly, Gregory was surprised to see the overgrown foliage opening up before them, allowing them to pass through with walls of tangled vegetation on both sides. He desperately wanted to ask the Grimbockle about it, but with the warning from the Guardbockle still ringing fresh in his ears, he remained silent.

They walked through the parted jungle for what seemed like hours to Gregory but in reality was only a short time. As they came out of the Brumbly, they entered a clearing. The first thing Gregory saw was giant floppy plants that looked a little like mushrooms. The heads of the plants were all packed closely together, and the surface of each was covered in hollow protrusions that reminded Gregory of the suckers on an octopus.

Underneath each of the mushroom plants grew clusters of silver trees, bony and leafless yet beautiful. In the midst of the trees, Bockles were hard at work sawing off some of the larger branches and grinding them into a fine silvery powder. As they passed by, all of the Bockles stopped their work to stare. Gregory thought they stared especially hard at him, and he crouched down a little deeper into the Grimbockle's pocket.

Further along the way, they came upon a funny looking house that was flat and round. In front of the house, a fat Bockle with a long, wavy beard was feeding scoopfuls of the collected powder into a noisy machine. Shimmering silver liquid poured out of a crystal pipe at the end and collected in a crystal bucket. A skinny Bockle stood by to replace the full bucket with an empty one, and a third Bockle took the full bucket, added a lid, and pasted on a SILVER SHRINKER label.

Gregory was beginning to enjoy the journey through Bocklia. Everything he saw was enchanting...even magical. After seeing how Silver Shrinker was made, he began to wonder about the other buckets of magical liquid, and just as he thought about the Carrot Juicy, he saw the biggest carrots he'd ever seen. They were like the trunks of trees with leaves spraying out the top like palm trees.

Eventually, they left the fields and forest and came to the mouth of a large cave. The cave was built into the wall of a colossal mountain—so high Gregory couldn't see the top. A deep ravine,

with only a narrow, arched bridge, lay between them and the entrance.

Gregory swallowed nervously as they approached the bridge, promising himself he wouldn't look down. Yet before they even set foot on it, he found he couldn't help himself. Stealing a quick glance, he looked down to where the ground dropped into the jagged ravine. Down at the very bottom, a golden river wound around like a serpent. Gregory's head swam, and he was immediately glad to be in the Grimbockle's pocket, where he felt at least a little safer.

As soon as they began crossing the bridge, the ravine vanished, and Gregory found himself looking at a peaceful golden river, bubbling just beneath them. On the banks of the river, what the Grimbockle told him were Shebockles were filling up crystal buckets with the label GOLDEN GROWER. The Shebockles were smaller than the other Bockles Gregory had seen so far, short and squat and buxom indeed. Their faces were set with rosy apple cheeks, and their hair seemed thicker and wilder than the Hebockles'. They, too, looked up curiously as the party passed them by.

The Grimbockle seemed nervous as they entered the cave, but Gregory was terrified. He could only imagine something awful living in such a dark, dank place. Just as he thought about closing his eyes, the darkness dispersed like a fog. Looking back, he could still see it hanging like a great black curtain, but everything before him was warm, dry, and light.

Gregory could see they had stepped into a brightly painted town. When he looked up at the Grimbockle, he saw a strange expression on its face. It seemed to be a mixture of guilt and relief, like a naughty child who had just come home from school with bad grades and was ready to confess.

Gregory could tell the Bockles were creative creatures, for the houses in the cave were built in every imaginable shape and painted in multiple colours. As they passed, Bockles came out their front doors and headed towards them, as if they had somehow all been notified of their arrival. Before long, there was a great procession following them.

As Gregory caught sight of more and more Bockles, he noticed a great variation in their shapes and sizes.

"Are they all Bockles?" he whispered up to the Grimbockle.

"Of course they is!" the Grimbockle hissed down at him, then looked quickly around to make sure the guards weren't paying attention.

"But...they're all so different!"

"How is you meaning?" asked the Grimbockle.

"They're all different shapes."

The Grimbockle shook his head at Gregory. "Hoo-mans is also in different shapes and sizes, is they not? But they is all still one and the same. All hoo-mans is hoo-mans just as all Bockles is Bockles.

The Grimbockle had a point, but even so, Gregory couldn't keep himself from gawking at all the uniquely formed Bockles on display as the Guardbockles marched them straight through town.

After some time, they reached a tall castle. The entire procession began making their way up a long, winding staircase, which wound round and round and seemed to go on forever.

Right when Gregory began to feel a little sick from all the winding, they came to the top and walked into a lavish room with a large jade throne sitting at the centre.

The Bockle seated on the throne watched them with a look of deep disapproval as they entered. Its skin was a brighter purple than any of the Bockles Gregory had seen. It was slightly larger than the Grimbockle and had a well-groomed beard that reached down to its rounded belly. It wore a glittering crown, carved from an opal. Like the rest of the Bockles, it had little clothing on—only a single golden cloth draped over one of its shoulders.

"Grrrimbockle!" it boomed in a loud voice.

"The Grandbockle," whispered the Grimbockle to Gregory with a catch in its throat.

From inside of its pocket, Gregory could feel the Grimbockle trembling, but it seemed frozen stiff at the same time. A Guardbockle gave it a nudge, and the Grimbockle began to move forward.

"Grrrimbockle!" the Grandbockle said, its voice echoing through the chamber again. "You is betterrr be getting over here now!"

The Guardbockles stood still, and the Grimbockle crept forward with its head hung low.

The Bockles, who had followed them from the town, stood behind them in a semicircle. They watched intently, making little noises of approval and disapproval, like a buzzing crowd waiting for a game of football to start.

"Grrrimbockle!" boomed the Grandbockle a third time. "I is hearrring frrrightsome foolish tales!"

Despite their current predicament, Gregory couldn't help but be delighted at the way the Grandbockle rolled its "r's" when it spoke.

"I is hearrring that you is sky-larrrking, here and there, with hoo-man kinds, whisperrring Bockle secrr-rets in their earrrlings and painting them with our paints, but I is not believing such hogwash until I is seeing it rrright this instant! Is you denying the trrruth, as I is seeing it before my only eyes?"

The Grimbockle was trembling so much, Gregory worried he'd rattle right out of its pocket.

"I is not denying any truths," the Grimbockle said with a shaky voice.

"Well, what is you doing, then? Has you gone brrroody as a bat? Is you abandoning your clear-thinking faculties?"

By now, the force of its speech had made the Grandbockle rise several inches off its throne, and it was glaring down at both of them so closely that Gregory could smell its breath, which strangely was not unpleasant at all. Rather like the smell of a fresh-cut capsicum. Still, it was very close, and at his current size, Gregory felt quite vulnerable, so he slid down lower into the Grimbockle's pocket.

"Is you keeping this hoo-man as a pet?" bellowed the Grandbockle.

"No! I is never doing such a thing!"

"Then what is you doing? And what is that

rrridiculous thing you is wearrring arrround your neck?"

The Grandbockle reached over and plucked the necklace straight off the Grimbockle's neck. He turned it over in his hands, carefully inspecting it, then sat down with a sigh.

"I is always suspecting we is sending you out much too soon after your trrraining," he said, shaking his head. "You is always having a pearrr-shaped passion for hoo-mans and their ways. I is never understanding it."

At this, the Grimbockle seemed to gather itself, and a fire crept into its eyes. "You is not understanding hoo-mans the way I is!"

"Piffle! I is understanding perrrfectly how hoo-mans is daily damaging exoodles, upstairrrs and down! It is why exoodles is in crrrises, is it not?"

"Not all hoo-mans is breaking exoodles. Some is even fixing them!"

When the Grimbockle said this, the crowd began to chatter madly, all at once, in disapproving tones.

"This is neverrr happening!" shrieked the Grandbockle. "Not in a million moons."

"It is! I is seeing it myself!"

"Never!" spat the Grandbockle.

During the last part of the discussion, the Grimbockle had seemed frustrated, but now, its face began to turn from purple to pink to scarlet.

The Grimbockle stood tall when he said, "I is seeing Gregor-ee drop a dark exoodle dead off another hoo-man's head!"

As soon as the words left its mouth, all the background chattering stopped, and the throne room was deadly quiet—so quiet, in fact, that Gregory could hear the Grimbockle's rapid breaths huffing in and out. Small as he was, Gregory could still feel all eyes in the room turn to him, and the air in the room shifted slightly, as if the entire crowd had leaned forward to catch the next words.

"Is it trrrue what he is saying?" croaked the Grandbockle, looking to Gregory. "Is you rrreally drrropping a dark exoodle dead as a doorrrpost?"

Gregory used the edge of the pocket to lift himself up a little higher. "Well," he began, "I didn't actually know what I was doing, and I'm still not sure how one little note could have done all that."

He said the last part more to himself than any-one else. Truthfully, the majority of the evening's events still made very little sense to Gregory. He was still trying to wrap his mind around exoo-dles and Bockles actually existing, never mind the slaying of dark exoodles.

"But is you rrresponsible for getting rrrid of it?" said the Grandbockle, with a note of urgency in its voice.

"Well," said Gregory, carefully, "it's hard to say. I didn't see the dark exoodles drop off. But, well, I suppose it is possible."

Until now, the Grandbockle had been looking fearsome and cross, but as soon as Gregory said this, it slumped backward into its throne like a balloon that had suddenly deflated. The room, which had been utterly quiet moments before, erupted into noisy chatter.

Eventually, the Grandbockle raised its hand for silence and spoke again. "You is hearrring how hoo-man exoodles is in parrrticularly dire straits?" it said, watching Gregory solemnly.

"Yes, the Grimbockle did mention something about things being in a bad way."

The Grandbockle gave a coarse laugh.

"A bad way is a gently way of putting it. Hoo-man exoodles is going bad long ago. It is why we is sent in the firrrst place. We is being sent to help keep exoodles sprrrightly and strrrong for all hoo-man kind."

"I think that's wonderful," said Gregory, feeling his mood begin to lift.

"No. It is not wonderful. I is saying we is *supposed* to be keeping exoodles sprrrightly and strrrong. I is not saying we is succeeding. We is not succeeding at all. We is actually failing."

A hush fell over the crowd again. Looking around, Gregory could see that long shadows had fallen across each of the peculiar faces around him, including the face of the Grimbockle. But the Grandbockle looked saddest of all.

Looking at the floor now, it said, "When we is first arrriving, we is being extrrremely successful. We is having to do hardly any work, and our work is bearrring lots of frrruits. Now, it is not so. Exoodles is all in dire straits and is falling off faster than flakes of skin. Bockles is never seeing anything like it beforrre. Then, suddenly, dark exoodles is crrropping up out of the nowheres, and Bockles is not knowing what to do about it. We is failing over and over again."

The Grandbockle seemed pained at its admission, and Gregory felt he must say something to comfort it.

"I'm sure you've all done the very best you could," he said. "You shouldn't be so hard on yourselves."

The Grandbockle looked up at Gregory, its huge eyes filled with shining tears. Its chin began to tremble, and its shoulders gave a shudder as it began to cry.

The Bockles (who were not at all accustomed to seeing the Grandbockle cry) immediately dissolved into tears as well. Gregory ducked down inside the Grimbockle's pocket. He was feeling sad for the Bockles and felt especially sad for the Grimbockle when one of its great tears splashed on top of his head.

Gregory waited until the Grimbockle wasn't crying so hard then said, "Grimbockle, I would very much like to be painted with some Golden Grower, if you don't mind."

The Grimbockle nodded, took Gregory out of its pocket, and set him down. Wiping away its tears, it pulled out the Golden Grower, and painted Gregory the same size as itself.

Gregory waited for the Grandbockle to compose itself before speaking again.

"The thing is," said Gregory, "you can't go fixing all the problems of the world yourselves. Let's put our heads together. I'm sure we can think of something to help the exoodles."

"I think you is rrright, little hoo-man," said the Grandbockle, sniffling—and smiling for the first time. "Grrrimbockle!"

The Grimbockle froze.

"I is misjudging you harrrshly," said the Grandbockle gently. "If it is how you say it is, perrrhaps we is needing to learn some things from this little hoo-man."

It finished its sentence with a flourish of its left hand, and out flew the Grimbockle's necklace, which landed magically back around its neck.

"I is commanding you to keep this hoo-man underrr your everrr watching eyes and to be finding out its magical ways."

"But I don't have any magical ways," Gregory said, feeling flustered.

"You is having morrre magic than you is knowing about," said the Grandbockle with a chuckle.

"Grrrimbockle, I is rrrelieving you from yourrr maintenance duties, and I is giving you a new job. You is going back with Grrregorrry, and you is watching daily what he is doing. I is wanting the bi-weekly rrreport of your happenings. But when you is coming home for your rrreporting, I is thinking it is better if you is leaving the hoo-man behind. I is impressed it is surrrviving its travels here in the first place, but we is maybe not being so lucky next time."

The Grandbockle looked directly at Gregory.

"Beforrre I is meeting you, I is not thinking about you being torrrn to bits, but now, I is thinking, and I is not wanting that to happen to you."

Before Gregory had a chance to speak, the Grandbockle produced a transporter pager exactly like the one that had brought them both to Bocklia and handed it to the Grimbockle.

The light started to spin around them. Faster and faster it spun until, once again, they were enveloped in a glowing circle of light.

Gregory heard the Grandbockle say, "I is glad I is meeting you, Grrregorrry. We is counting on you, little hoo-man."

Just as he began to reply, a loud rushing sound filled Gregory's ears. Then came the same uncomfortable sucking sensation.

Eventually, the two of them tumbled straight out of the air together and landed in a messy little pile back where they had started: on the table in Tommy's bedroom. Like a puppy excited to see its master, the cockroach creature pounced as soon as it saw them, nuzzling, jumping, and making small, pleased clicking sounds.

"We is fine, we is," said the Grimbockle, trying to convince the cockroach. But still, it circled around sniffing and nuzzling, making it clear it had missed its master. Once the cockroach had calmed down, the Grimbockle painted them so they were all ant-sized, then climbed back onto its faithful steed, pulled Gregory up, and set off on the Exoodle Expressway. Gregory cast a final glance back at Tommy, who was sleeping peacefully with a gentle smile touching the corners of his mouth.

As they careened along, Gregory noticed the sun beginning to rise. A thin orange veil of predawn light touched the sky, and the Exoodle Expressway began to glow. It glittered and sparkled, picking up the colours around it, taking Gregory's breath away.

Before he knew it, Gregory was back in his room.

"I think we is done for tonight," said the Grimbockle, looking sleepy.

Gregory started to feel a little sad about the

adventure coming to an end, but then, a sudden wave of tiredness hit him. With all the speeding up and slowing down of time, he had no idea how long they'd been gone, but as it was, he was barely able to keep his eyes open.

The Grimbockle pulled out his Golden Grower and said, "We is better be painting you back to your original size, or your family is all having rude shocks when they is waking up."

Gregory gave a chuckle at the image of his mother finding him in bed in the morning, no bigger than an insect.

"Yes, I suppose that would be shocking."

Once he was back to his normal size, Gregory hobbled over to his bed and crawled under the blankets. He couldn't ever remember being so tired.

"How on earth will I stay awake in school tomorrow?" he wondered aloud.

"You is not needing to worry," said the Grimbockle, who had galloped up on the cockroach and was now standing beside the pillow where Gregory could see it. "You is forgetting I has this," it said, producing the dial scromple from out of its side pocket. "I is slowing down time now, nice and slow, so you is getting at least forty winks. Maybe more."

"That sounds wonderful," said Gregory, burrowing deep in his pillow.

Right before he drifted off to sleep, he became vaguely aware of something creeping up his cheek and moving to the space above his lip. He opened one eye, just in time to see the Grimbockle and the cockroach disappear into his mole.

"Goodnight Gregor-ee," it whispered, letting the mole fall gently shut over the top of it, like a trapdoor in the floor.

"Goodnight," whispered Gregory to the darkness.

CHAPTER 11

Exoodle Work

Morning finally came, but even after a long, deep sleep, when his alarm clock rang Gregory didn't stir. It wasn't until his mother came in at half past eight and yanked his blankets off that he finally woke up.

Marjory, who was already dressed for school, stood snickering at him from the doorway. "Time to get up, lazybones," she said.

"Really, Gregory!" scolded his mother.

As they trailed out of his room, Gregory shivered and curled into a ball. His body was stiff and sore, and without his blanket, the morning air felt much too cold. He considered pulling the blankets back up, but instead, he forced himself to get up.

As he searched for something to wear, the grogginess of sleep cleared, and the events of the night came rushing back to him. When he remembered the Grimbockle, he gently placed a finger on his mole. It felt no different than usual, and Gregory wondered if he had dreamt it all.

But no. Not only did he feel a hundred years old, but also there, on his floor, was the mess of dominos, which had all fallen flat. Just as this evidence confirmed his thought, he felt a sudden twitching at his mole. He rushed over to the mirror just in time to see the Grimbockle's head peeking out, as if he were looking out of a window.

Even at this size, Gregory could plainly see the guilt written across its face as it surveyed the fallen dominos. Gregory gave a sigh and picked one up, wondering how long it would take to set so many up again.

"We is sorry we is knocking down all your dominos, Gregor-ee. We is never meaning to. Perhaps we is helping you stacking them up again?"

"It's okay," said Gregory, putting the domino down.

Truthfully, Gregory didn't want to spend all that time alone again stacking dominos. Besides, now that he was back, he knew there was work to be done, and it wasn't going to be easy. Since having his eyes painted with Carrot Juicy and seeing for himself the frailness of his family exoodles, he'd become quite bothered.

Even though they'd drifted apart, Gregory remembered a time when they had enjoyed picnics, played board games, hiked, gardened, and gone on fishing trips together. Now, they only seemed to share a home...not their lives. Although he had gotten used to things being as they were, he missed his family and knew he needed to try to fix things.

He also knew he couldn't change everything all at once, but he was determined to do everything he could to strengthen the exoodles that joined him to his mother, his father, and even his annoying older sister.

Gregory began helping his mother with the dishes at night and placing his father's slippers in the entryway so his feet wouldn't be cold on the tiles when he got home from work. He even offered to help Marjory with her chores. (She was so shocked, she couldn't think of a single insult to say to him the entire time.) He kept on like this, helping where he could and doing nice little things for all of them—even when he didn't feel like it.

Nothing happened right away, but as all the little things added up over the weeks, Gregory saw the exoodles between him and his family begin to heal. They grew thicker and more vibrant every day.

The Grimbockle did little but follow Gregory around most days, exactly as the Grandbockle had ordered it. Some days, it stayed inside Gregory's mole; other days, it hid up in his hair; and occasionally, it would go inside the breast pocket of his school uniform blazer. Now and then, it would disappear for days, reporting back to Bocklia, but most days they spent together, and as the weeks rolled by, Gregory and the Grimbockle grew quite fond of each other. (Though Gregory couldn't quite seem to get used to it popping in and out of his mole like a jack-in-the-box.)

Gregory found he could no longer look at moles the same way. He couldn't help but stare whenever he saw an especially large one, wondering if there was a Bockle living inside and hoping he might spot one. In fact, for a while, he became so preoccupied with this strange activity that his grades began to suffer, so his mole watching soon came to an end. Instead, he began watching exoodles, which took much less concentration.

Seeing exoodles not only made Gregory mindful of his own family relations, but also helped him build two new friendships at school (though they hadn't at all been with the kinds of people Gregory would have expected to be friends with).

First, there was Jamie. She was a quiet girl with bright red hair and pale skin absolutely peppered with freckles. Before he had been able to see the exoodles, Gregory thought of Jamie the same way the rest of the class did. Quiet and a little geeky—the kind of girl who preferred to go out to the mulberry tree at recess and watch lizards rather than play basketball with the other kids in the yard. But when he had returned to school after his evening with the Grimbockle, Gregory had been utterly mystified to find that quiet, geeky Jamie had more exoodles coming from her than anyone else in the class...good strong exoodles glowing with strength and light. He remembered then the Grimbockle saying, "Freckly hoomans is always delightful and is always making lots of exoodles quickly with everyone in sight."

True enough, as soon as Gregory was paired with Jamie for a science project, an exoodle reached out to him, and they instantly became friends.

More surprising than his blossoming friendship with Jamie was his friendship with Ted. Ted was an exceptionally bright boy in their class who continued to score the highest grades with seemingly no effort at all. This should have made him quite popular with the rest of the class, except it didn't. Ted was a rude boy who had a knack for saying things in a specifically irritating way. In fact, it often seemed like Ted enjoyed mocking and ridiculing his classmates.

One day, when they had a spelling test, Gregory accidentally spelled the word, "kite" with a "y." He didn't feel too bad about it until Ted leaned over his shoulder and said, "Even my little sister can spell that one," which made his classmates laugh, and then Gregory did care.

Gregory wasn't surprised to see that Ted had barely any exoodles at all. What did surprise him was what had happened one day during a pop quiz in math.

It was the end of the day, but the teacher had set a very difficult question on the blackboard. Gregory knew he hadn't done the homework required for the question and therefore had no clue how to answer it, but even so, he felt compelled to stare hard at the space in front of him and nibble at the tip of his pencil as if he were trying to solve it anyway. Eventually, he found himself absentmindedly inspecting the exoodles of the person at the desk in front of him. That person was Ted.

He saw a few large exoodles hanging limply from his sides. They weren't in terrible shape, but Gregory knew now that limp exoodles weren't healthy ones. Healthy exoodles hung high in the air, pulsing gently on mysterious otherworldly currents. Limp exoodles, such as these, would slowly decay over time if nothing was done to heal them.

Remembering the spelling test incident, Gregory huffed under his breath and thought, *He deserves to have sickly exoodles*. But just when he thought it, he noticed something peculiar. Tiny exoodle threads, so thin he'd never noticed them before, reached out from Ted in fragile tendrils by the hundreds. They seemed to be desperately reaching out to everyone but were unable to attach.

Right then, Miss Weatherington came by and thrust Gregory's head back down to face his desk. He was left to stare at his blank paper and wonder about the unusual, tiny exoodle threads attached to Ted.

When the test was finished, Miss Weatherington had Ted collect all the papers as the students left through the classroom door. Ted had smart remarks for all of them.

"Nice handwriting, Hendrickson."

"Did you fall asleep and dribble on your paper, Bradley?"

When Gregory was passing through Ted said, "Bet you flunked that one."

Gregory opened his mouth to say something rude but then noticed one of the delicate exoodles reaching out to him from Ted. It suddenly struck him... *Could Ted possibly be using rude remarks to try to make friends?*

To test his theory, Gregory offered Ted a warm smile and said, "Yeah, I shouldn't expect to pass since I didn't study. I'm sure you'll get a good grade though."

As Gregory walked through the doorway, Ted watched him curiously but said nothing.

The next morning, when Gregory woke up, he found a silvery thread attached to his ear, and that was the beginning of his friendship with Ted.

It wasn't easy at first, but Gregory quickly realised Ted wasn't bad at all; he only wanted some friends.

An exoodle had stretched out from easygoing Jamie to Ted in no time, and the three became inseparable with strong, healthy exoodles quivering joyfully between them.

CHAPTER 12

Old Ethel

One day, while Gregory walked home from school, the Grimbockle rode on his ear, chattering, "He is a horrid boy before! Just horrid! But Gregor-ee is changing Ted, and now he is having all kinds of newfound friends! And your family relations is being better, and the exoodles is growing stronger between you...."

On and on the Grimbockle chittered, eventually bringing up, once again (for the Grimbockle was especially proud of this moment), the way Gregory had stopped the dark exoodle "dead as a doorpost."

Gregory never grew tired of the delightful

way the Grimbockle spoke. Its voice was like a brook bubbling in his ear, which made it difficult to notice anything else—like old Ethel hiding behind the crab-apple tree waiting to pounce. Just as he moved past her house, she snuck up on him, sprang forward like a gazelle, and plucked his mole right off his face.

When it first happened, Gregory bellowed and howled like a wounded beast, but after a moment passed, he realised it actually didn't hurt at all and, in fact, wasn't even bleeding. It seemed that, after being plucked at and scrubbed so many times, his sad little mole had only been hanging by a thread.

From an aesthetic point of view, Gregory wasn't particularly sorry to see it go, but even so, it was rather rude to just pluck someone's mole off. As he inspected the area with his fingers, Gregory found that the skin was smooth and soft where his mole had been. This surprised him more than anything else, for he'd expected there to be some evidence of the Grimbockle living there.

Gregory suddenly felt butterflies fluttering in his stomach and worried about the Grimbockle.

Where will it live? he wondered.

Feeling angry at the thought of old Ethel ruining the Grimbockle's home, he turned around ready to give her the tongue lashing of her life, but something stopped him. For there, on top of her head, was a mass of ugly, twisted dark exoodles, writhing about like hundreds of gruesome, slithering serpents.

Gregory stiffened when he saw them and heard the Grimbockle whimper up by his ear. Seeing he wasn't going to put up a fight, old Ethel gave a disappointed grunt, then wandered off back inside her house, leaving Gregory and the Grimbockle dazed.

"Ohhh!" said the Grimbockle, sounding faint. "Never in my whiskered millenniums is I ever seeing something so foulsome as I is seeing now! So many dark exoodles, crawling and squiggling! I is having a five-legged fit! I is melting down like ice in the sun! I is not even knowing my top from my bottom!"

It staggered a little, holding tightly to the hair above Gregory's ear so it wouldn't fall off.

"I think I've seen them on her before," said

Gregory in a quiet voice.

"You isn't meaning it?"

"I think I is. Am!" said Gregory, correcting himself. "It was on the night I first met you. I remember flying over old Ethel's house and seeing something in her hair, but we went by so quickly...."

"Oh, my trembling rump!" cried the Grimbockle. "Oh, my sweet liver dandies! I is not even knowing where to begin."

"Well, we can't leave things the way they are, can we?" said Gregory, sounding much more positive than he felt. "Otherwise, old Ethel will wind up infecting everyone around her with her dark exoodles."

"You is having a plan?" said the Grimbockle hopefully.

"Maybe." Gregory wasn't sure.

The Grimbockle perked up and looked at him intently.

"Gregor-ee is coming up with a plan, is he not?"

But Gregory hadn't gotten that far yet. He was still mulling it all around in his head. He wasn't certain he wanted to help old Ethel. Perhaps she was simply a nasty old cow who deserved to have those dark exoodles swimming in her hair.

But another part of him felt sorry for her, so he decided to approach the matter exactly the same way he had with Tommy and his mother. He would write a note.

CHAPTER 13

Fresh Baked Biscuits

Dear Ethel,
I just wanted to say thank you for managing
to pluck that mole off my face. It's been both-
ering me for some time, and I'm very glad to
be rid of it.
Your neighbour,
Gregory

He wasn't being entirely honest. Because of the Grimbockle, Gregory was quite sad about his mole being gone, but it was all he could think of for now, and he figured it was better than nothing.

He looked over the note one last time before depositing it into the mailbox. As he walked away, he began thinking about the Grimbockle and wondered where it would sleep that night. The Grimbockle, however, seemed to be perfectly content sleeping in the tufts of Gregory's hair, saying, "Sleeping in Gregor-ee's hair is like sleeping in the sweet barn hay."

When the weekend arrived, Gregory was a little upset with himself, because he hadn't yet thought of anything else to do for Ethel. He lay awake for a while that Friday night, wondering if there was any hope for her, and eventually he drifted off to sleep. He awoke the next morning to the glorious smell of freshly baking biscuits wafting through his bedroom door.

He sprung out of bed and stumbled into the kitchen, still half asleep.

"Morning, Greg," said his father, walking back to the table with a fresh cup of coffee. He ruffled Gregory's hair as he passed by in a way he hadn't done in years.

Gregory enjoyed the show of affection, though he did hope the Grimbockle had managed to get out of the way.

"Morning, Big Foot," said Marjory with a chuckle.

Out of habit, Gregory poked his tongue out at her, but he realised he was no longer offended by the nickname. Perhaps it was because Marjory said it differently now.

His mother had just pulled out a fresh tray of biscuits from the oven and was starting to lift them off onto the cooling rack with a spatula. Looking at the biscuits now, Gregory knew exactly what he needed to do, but before he could go anywhere, his mother insisted they all sit around the table and have breakfast like a family for once. Gregory couldn't even remember the last time they had shared a meal together.

His mother had also made pancakes, and they were dripping in butter and maple syrup, exactly the way Gregory liked them. It was a lovely breakfast indeed, and as they laughed and chattered, Gregory watched the exoodles humming happily between them.

By the time they were finished, Gregory was utterly stuffed. Just as he was ready to leave the

kitchen, he remembered his plan and asked his mother for a few more biscuits. She gave him a funny look and said, "Haven't you eaten enough?" But she packed them anyway, shaking her head and muttering something about the madness of growing boys and their appetites.

"Gregory," said his mother suddenly as he was walking out, "whatever happened to your mole?"

Grabbing his face, she twisted it about, as if she might find the mole had moved to a different place. Mumbling a vague excuse under his breath that didn't make any sense at all, Gregory quickly scampered off, leaving his mother utterly bewildered in the kitchen. He didn't want to lie to her, but he didn't want old Ethel getting into trouble, either.

Clutching his package of freshly baked biscuits, he practically sprinted out the door and down the street.

"Where is we going, Gregor-ee?" said the Grimbockle, popping up out of his hair.

"I have an idea," said Gregory.

"I *knew* Gregor-ee is thinking of something," said the Grimbockle gleefully.

Gregory had been hoping to simply leave the biscuits on the porch and ring the doorbell, but when he arrived at Ethel's house, he found she was out on the patio in her rocking chair, staring hard at the table in front of her.

She was so absorbed in whatever was on the table she hadn't even noticed Gregory, who was now standing no more than an arm's length away from her.

"Um...," said Gregory, clearing his throat a little.

Ethel said nothing but raised a single finger for silence and continued to focus on the table.

Gregory sighed quietly, thinking perhaps this hadn't been a good idea after all. He wondered what could be on the table to require such ardent attention and craned his neck forward a little to have a better look.

As soon as he saw what it was, Gregory gasped.

For what lay spread out on the table was none other than his favourite game in all the world. Dominos.

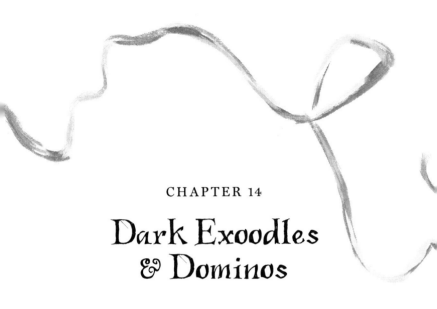

CHAPTER 14

Dark Exoodles & Dominos

Gregory had never seen dominos set up the way they were in front of Ethel.

"What are you doing with them?" he said aloud, his curiosity taking over.

"Hmph!" grunted old Ethel. "Nothing a young whippersnapper like yourself would be interested in."

"But I am interested," said Gregory. "I play with dominos all the time. It's one of my favourite things to do."

Ethel turned her head toward Gregory and seemed to be studying him. When she saw him staring curiously at the dominos, she said, "It's called Tiddly-Wink."

Turning her head back to the table, she picked up a tile and continued.

"It's supposed to be played by two or more, but an old bird like me knows how to play it just fine by myself!"

"How do you play?" said Gregory with a spark in his eyes.

In spite of herself, old Ethel started to soften a little and began to explain all the rules. When she was finished, and Gregory still seemed eager to play, she invited him to join her in a game.

Playing Tiddly-Wink with old Ethel was great fun for Gregory—much more interesting than just lining the tiles up and then knocking them down himself. Now and then, he would catch sight of the dark exoodles in Ethel's hair and find it rather unsettling, but playing dominos and sharing biscuits with her proved an excellent distraction.

Before he knew it, the day was gone, the biscuits had all been eaten, and it was time for Gregory to make his way home.

Before he left, old Ethel pressed a small paper bag into his hand. He started to open it, but she stopped him and shoved him off.

Realising how long he'd been gone, he hurried home. As soon as he walked through the door, his mother said, "Where on earth have you been, Gregory?"

Gregory hadn't heard real concern in his mother's voice over his absence in so long, he'd forgotten what it felt like. He rather liked the feeling.

"I've been with old Ethel," he said.

His sister, who was just in the other room, came rushing in.

"That old witch? You have not! You're terri-fied of her!"

"Well, she's not as bad as I thought. Besides, she likes dominos," said Gregory with a shrug.

"That's a lie. I bet you're hiding a girlfriend!"

Gregory rolled his eyes at that.

"I have proof," he said holding out his paper bag. "She gave me this when I was leaving."

Gregory opened up the bag a little reluc-tantly, not knowing what would be inside. They all peeked in as he held it open. He was happy to see soft caramel candies inside.

"See," he said proudly.

"They're probably filled with poison...or *cursed*!" said Marjory as she walked away laughing.

"Oh, go on and do your homework," her mother scolded.

Gregory's mother took a caramel out of the bag and said, "Rumour has it old Ethel won a blue rib-bon for those cara-mels years ago."

Gregory smiled at

that and wished Marjory had still been standing there when his mother had said it.

"Well, come and get your dinner, then," his mother said before stealing another caramel from Gregory's bag. "I kept it warm for you."

When Gregory was in bed that night, he asked the Grimbockle, "Will Marjory always be so annoying?"

The Grimbockle gave a chuckle. "Brothers and sisters is always annoying each other to the ends of the earth, even if their exoodles is springy and strong."

Gregory sighed but found comfort in the Grimbockle's words. Nobody knew how to irritate him the way Marjory did, but he knew, despite this, he loved her anyway.

The following day, Gregory went back to old Ethel's to play dominos again. He dropped by Monday after school as well, and by the time he arrived on Tuesday afternoon, she was waiting for him with a mug of hot chocolate and some freshly baked madeleines, which were quite delicious.

Before long, Gregory realised it was no longer

just about finding a way to destroy the dark exoodles. He visited Ethel because he actually enjoyed spending time with her. She was the only one who loved dominos as much as he did (and it didn't hurt that she always had a supply of freshly baked goodies for him to enjoy).

For a few months, things continued as they were. Gregory went to school, laughed with his friends, and played dominos with old Ethel in the afternoons. He begged the Grimbockle to take him on another adventure across the sea to fix exoodles again, but the Grimbockle was adamant that this would be against the Grandbockle's orders, which he seemed painfully conscious of since their return from Bocklia.

Several weeks later, on a particularly nice day, Gregory was playing dominos with Ethel. They were in the middle of an exceptionally challenging game when in the corner of his eye he thought he saw something fall from Ethel's head.

Gregory's eyes widened, and he could feel the Grimbockle startle within his hair. He looked down to discover that one of the dark exoodles had dropped from Ethel's head onto the ground, where it was writhing pitifully and shrivelling before his eyes. When it happened, Ethel placed a hand up to her head gently, almost as if she'd felt it fall off.

That night, when Gregory had been asleep for a few hours, the Grimbockle popped out of his hair and said, "Wake up, Gregor-ee. We is heading out on the Exoodle Expressway."

Gregory woke quickly. He had been itching for an adventure for ages.

The cockroach steed seemed overjoyed to be out as well and scuttled twice the speed it had before, getting them over to Ethel's in no time at all.

Though it was well past midnight, old Ethel was still up, hunched over the fireplace, staring sadly into the embers as she had been on Gregory's first adventure.

As soon as they arrived, it was plain to see something was afoot with the dark exoodles on her head. They were standing out on their ends, like the spikes of a porcupine, but quivering and trembling like freshly set jelly.

Gregory felt a pang in his heart as he watched Ethel, but just as he opened his mouth to ask the Grimbockle why the dark exoodles

were behaving so strangely, Gregory saw something he never expected to see. Crusty old Ethel began to cry.

Tears flowed down her cheeks, but they weren't normal tears. They were black at first and seemed to be getting clearer as they poured out from her eyes.

The dark exoodles were twisting and pulling exactly the way Tommy's had. It looked agonising, and right when Gregory wondered how Ethel could stand it, her head exploded into a beautiful, silvery-white light. It was more piercing than any light Gregory had ever seen—so bright he had to turn away from it—yet, in the presence of that light, Gregory felt enriched and alive.

When he looked back, squinting into the brightness, he could see the dark exoodles on Ethel's head, pointing out at their ends, paralysed by the light. They retracted for a moment, wrapping themselves in a foul, wriggling nest around Ethel's head. Her face grew dark for a moment, and the dark exoodles began to swell, bigger and stronger, pulsating with a dark, ominous glow.

All of a sudden, the silvery light grew brighter,

and the dark exoodles seemed to panic. Unwrapping themselves from old Ethel's head, they sprang outwards again, twisting and shrieking, like horrible weeds trying to pull themselves up out of the ground. Their mouths gasped open and shut, like breathless sea creatures washed up on the sand. Finally, all at once, the dark exoodles fell from Ethel's head.

She seemed to feel it, for Ethel's shoulders gave a little shiver, and she wrapped her shawl more tightly around her. She surprised Gregory next by bursting into laughter. It was a deep, bellyaching laugh that shook her stomach and made her give off a little snort now and then. She laughed and laughed until tears of a different kind were streaming down her face. These tears were shining clear and bright like precious jewels.

The Grimbockle's big eyes were even bigger than usual. "I is having to report this right away!" it said.

It handed a bucket of Golden Grower to Gregory, pulled out its transporter pager, and disappeared with flurry of red light and a... *pop*. Gregory took one last look at Ethel (who had fallen asleep), then climbed up onto the cockroach steed and headed back home.

Once he was back to full size and under his covers, Gregory lay there thinking about everything that had happened, and he chuckled when he realised how bonking mad everyone would think he was if he ever attempted to tell his story...which he wouldn't.

He waited up for the Grimbockle but then couldn't keep his eyes open and eventually drifted off to sleep.

Two hours later, when his mother stormed in, ripped off his blankets, and scolded, "Get up! You're late for school!" Gregory dearly wished the Grimbockle had thought to leave him with the dial scromple.

CHAPTER 15

Goodbyes

A week passed with no sign of the Grimbockle. Gregory worried it might not be coming back, but then he realised he still had the Golden Grower and, more importantly, the Grimbockle's cockroach steed.

Without the Grimbockle, it was difficult to keep the cockroach steed safe, and Gregory's mother very nearly murdered it one Tuesday night when she came in to wax the furniture in Gregory's bedroom. Luckily, Gregory managed to secret the little creature inside his pants pocket while his mother was looking the other way.

After that incident, he kept the cockroach in

the crater of the papier-mâché volcano he'd made for a class diorama and fed it crackers and raisins. He knew it would be safe there until the Grimbockle returned.

One night, Gregory lay awake thinking about the Grimbockle when a red light began whizzing about on the table beside him. He stared at it, desperately hoping it was the Grimbockle returning. When the light vanished, Gregory was delighted to see the Grimbockle had indeed returned but surprised to see the Grandbockle standing there, too.

As soon as the Grandbockle spotted Gregory, it burst into great sobbing tears. "Oh! I is a terrrible Bockle. I is a foul, sourrr milky kind!"

Gregory wasn't quite sure what to make of the situation. He looked to the Grimbockle for an explanation, but the Grimbockle seemed distracted by something at its feet.

The Grandbockle went on. "I is thinking so often that hoo-mans is horrrible exoodle wreckers, but Grrregorrree is nothing like this at all! You is actually helping us! You is even doing a better job than we is!"

The Grandbockle broke down utterly then and did nothing but sob for a full minute. In spite of its tears, Gregory couldn't help smiling a little, for he found it very endearing what an emotional little creature the Grandbockle was.

Eventually, it composed itself and said, "Lately, we is having oodles of meetings and discussings. We is having oodles of meetings about exoodles and oodles of meetings about hoo-mans as well. It is taking some time, but eventually, we is coming to an oh-so imporrrtant decision."

It paused for a moment to clear its throat and then went on. "After we is seeing cerrrtain things, we is rrrealising that we is no longer needed for helping with hoo-man exoodles, and we is deciding that we is betterrr moving on."

The Grimbockle, who had been strangely quiet this entire time, now looked positively miserable. Gregory felt miserable, too. "What will we do without you?" he said to the Grimbockle, his voice thick.

"You is needing to keep exoodle threads bonny and bouncy on your own two feets now," said the Grimbockle, unable to look at Gregory. "Ever since we is watching Gregor-ee's comings and goings, we is realising that hoo-mans is quite capable of their own exoodle maintenancing."

Gregory put his hand out for the Grimbockle, then lifted it up so that they were face-to-face. Finally, the Grimbockle looked up at him, a tear dropping from one of its large black eyes.

"But where will you go?" said Gregory, feeling sad.

"Other places is needing us. But you is not needing to worry. We is still checking in on

hoo-mans now and then, and I is checking in on you from time to time as well."

"Grrrimbockle. We is going," said the Grandbockle, its eyes still wet with tears. "I is not liking long goodbyes."

It quickly pulled out its dial scromple, and for the last time, the lights began to whizz and blur.

"We is having many happy times together," said the Grimbockle. "I is never forgetting them."

It gave Gregory's thumb a final squeeze as he set it back down onto the table, and soon, there were two little flashing spheres of light.

Watching them leave, Gregory could feel a lump forming in his throat, when he suddenly remembered the cockroach hiding inside his volcano.

"Grimbockle! Wait!" he cried.

Inside the paper crater, the cockroach steed was scuttling about furiously, desperate to get out. Gregory quickly scooped it up and deposited it gently inside the Grimbockle's ball of light just before it disappeared.

"Goodbye, Gregor-ee!" came the Grimbockle's voice one last time as they vanished.

"Goodbye, Grimbockle," whispered Gregory.

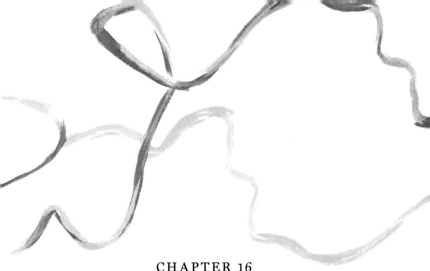

CHAPTER 16

Life Without Bockles

G regory hardly slept at all that night. He spent a good portion of the night clicking the KEENVIZZ 8000 on and off, on and off... scanning the room in hope the Grimbockle would appear.

When his mother entered his room in the morning, he was lying awake, staring at the ceiling. She sat on the edge of his bed and said, "Everything okay?"

"Hmm?" he grunted.

His mother stared at him a moment as if wondering how far to probe. "Well," she said finally, "keeping a secret or two from your old mumsie is fine—so long as you know I'm always here if you need me."

Gregory sat up and looked curiously at his mother.

"Okay?" she said with a reassuring nod.

Feeling a sudden rush of happiness, Gregory smiled at his mother and nodded back.

When his mother left, Marjory walked by the open door. "Out of bed, sleepy sloth moth!" she said, moving towards the kitchen.

His dad even popped his head in and said, "See you later, Greg!"

A couple moments later, Marjory returned, standing in the doorway with her hands behind her back. Gregory eyed her suspiciously. Before he could ask her what she was doing, she whipped out a breakfast plate from behind her back. It held fried eggs, bacon, and two pieces of buttered toast, just the way Gregory liked it (toast cooled with unmelted butter spread thickly on top). Gregory opened his mouth to thank her, but Marjory hurried out before he had a chance, leaving Gregory to his breakfast.

Gregory was shocked. He was used to quiet mornings alone, not greetings from every family member, and certainly not his sister delivering his breakfast. It all felt so strange...and wonderful.

Remembering the Grimbockle's penchant for human things, Gregory wished he could offer it some bacon. He felt sad for a moment, but then he looked at his plate and cheered up a little. After all, one couldn't be too sad with a hot plate of crisp bacon and eggs waiting to be eaten.

With the Grimbockle gone, Gregory expected to feel lonely, but it was hard to feel too lonely with his new friends, Jamie and Ted. They were coming over regularly now, and twice a week, they even went with him to old Ethel's to play dominos.

Ethel taught them all kinds of new games— Block and Draw, Maltese Cross, and even Chicken Foot (for which Gregory would have to recruit a few extra players).

Even with newly formed exoodles, there was always a dark mark on Ethel's head that looked like a tree had been dug out, but of course, only

Gregory was ever able to see it, because his eyes had been painted with the Carrot Juicy.

As soon as he was old enough, Gregory got himself a job at a local factory where he saved himself a handsome sum. Then he set out to see the world. For he had never forgotten the Grimbockle's words: *"Travel is strengthening great many other bits and bobbles in hoo-mans."*

Gregory met many people and made all kinds of new friends as he travelled the world, but eventually he made his way back home, where he married and had two children of his own.

Just as paint on a house slowly fades with time, so, too, did the Carrot Juicy that had been painted over Gregory's eyes, and the ability to see the exoodles diminished greatly over time. Yet somehow, just knowing exoodles were there made Gregory work twice as hard to form count-less new threads over his lifetime. In the end, Gregory was an exceptionally happy, well-loved man with dozens of strong, sprightly threads, quivering with health and life.

Throughout his lifetime, Gregory never forgot the Grimbockle. His children and grandchildren grew up hearing stories of Bockles, pink suns, feathery trees, buckets of magic, dial scromples, and cockroach travel—but most importantly... about the mysterious exoodle threads living amongst us, moving in the corners of our eyes, and connecting us all to one another.

Bios

AUTHOR: Melanie Schubert is a scriptwriter and songwriter for the New Zealand performing arts company, Gobsmacked. She lives in a small, cosy apartment with her beloved husband Filip, a shelf of books and a peculiar assortment of Japanese paraphernalia. For as long as she can remember, she has been staring out of windows, losing herself in daydreams, and pursuing her belief that she must carve out and follow her own path in life.

ILLUSTRATOR: Abigail Kraft is forever nine years old, believes in magic, and likes to draw pictures. She has decided, a childish spirit is her favorite avenue to creativity, so she fills her days with music, family, giggles, daydreams, and animated movies. Then (in true, childish fashion) she cries, grumbles, and sighs her way through unpleasant work, and shows her mom as soon as she's made something she's proud of. Most of all, she loves her Creator, who gave her a super fun life and promises her eternity in the most funnest place of all.

COMPOSER: Jared Kraft is a composer for film and media. His passion for music began with experience through listening, moved to expression through piano and eventually arrived at creation through composition. He finds his purpose and inspiration in his perfect Savior, his loving wife, and his wonderful family, and will always value the timeless phenomenon in which organized noise is translated into a universal language.

Acknowledgements

I would like to thank the team at New Wrinkle—Lynnette, Jared, Abigail, and all of the invisible members behind the scenes, for seeing something in my work and sharing the vision of my weird and warped mind. I would especially like to thank Lynnette for working tirelessly with me to turn my raw manuscript into something slightly more coherent.

And lastly but by no means least, I would like to thank my darling husband Filip, who has believed in me always and continues to be my greatest support and number one fan.

CPSIA information can be obtained
at www.ICGtesting.com
Printed in the USA
LVOW10s1809080518
576442LV00009B/663/P